THE HONJIN MURDERS

SEISHI YOKOMIZO (1902–81) was one of Japan's most famous and best-loved mystery writers. He was born in Kobe and spent his childhood reading detective stories, before beginning to write stories of his own, the first of which was published in 1921. He went on to become an extremely prolific and popular author, best known for his Kosuke Kindaichi series, which ran to 77 books, many of which were adapted for stage and television in Japan. *The Honjin Murders* is the first Kosuke Kindaichi story, and regarded as one of Japan's great mystery novels. It won the first Mystery Writers of Japan Award in 1948 but has never been translated into English, until now. *The Inugami Curse*, *The Village of Eight Graves*, *Death on Gokumon Island* and *The Devil's Flute Murders* are also available from Pushkin Vertigo.

LOUISE HEAL KAWAI grew up in Manchester, UK but Japan has been her home since 1990. She previously translated Soji Shimada's *Murder in the Crooked House* and Mieko Kawakami's *Ms Ice Sandwich* for Pushkin Press. Her other translations include *Seventeen* by Hideo Yokoyama and Seicho Matsumoto's *A Quiet Place*.

THE HONJIN MURDERS

PUSHKIN VERTIGO

Seishi Yokomizo

TRANSLATED BY LOUISE HEAL KAWAI

Pushkin Press
Somerset House, Strand
London WC2R 1LA

HONJIN SATSUJIN JIKEN

© Seishi YOKOMIZO 1973

First published in Japan in 1973 by KADOKAWA CORPORATION, Tokyo.

English translation rights arranged with KADOKAWA CORPORATION, Tokyo through JAPAN UNI AGENCY, INC., Tokyo.

English translation © Louise Heal Kawai 2019

First published by Pushkin Press in 2019

13

ISBN 13: 978-1-78227-500-8

All rights reserved. No part of this publication may be reproduced, stored in a retrieval system or transmitted in any form or by any means, electronic, mechanical, photocopying, recording or otherwise, without prior permission in writing from Pushkin Press

Designed and typeset by Tetragon, London
Printed and bound by Clays Ltd, Elcograf S.p.A.

www.pushkinpress.com

CONTENTS

CHARACTER LIST

THE ICHIYANAGI FAMILY

Itoko	*the family matriarch, widowed*
Kenzo	*the eldest son and bridegroom*
Taeko	*the elder daughter, living in Shanghai*
Ryuji	*the second son, doctor in Osaka*
Saburo	*the third son, currently unemployed*
Suzuko	*the younger daughter, considered "a bit slow"*
Ryosuke	*cousin of Kenzo and his siblings, manages the family finances*
Akiko	*Ryosuke's wife*
Ihei	*great-uncle of Kenzo and Ryosuke; younger brother of Sakue and Hayato's father*
(Sakue	*deceased husband of Itoko, and father of five)*
(Hayato	*deceased brother of Sakue, and father of Ryosuke)*

THE KUBO FAMILY

Katsuko	*bride and schoolteacher in Okayama City*
Ginzo	*uncle of the bride, successful fruit farmer*
(Rinkichi	*father of Katsuko, and brother of Ginzo)*
Shizuko Shiraki	*friend of Katsuko's*

SERVANTS

Kiyo	*maid*
Nao	*servant / cook*
Genshichi	*servant / farmworker*
Shokichi	*servant / farmworker*

POLICE OFFICERS

Detective Inspector Isokawa
Detective Sergeant Kimura
Chief Inspector

PRIVATE DETECTIVE

Kosuke Kindaichi

Various police officers, farmworkers and other minor characters

CHAPTER 1

The Three-Fingered Man

Before recording the strange history that follows, I felt I ought to take a look at the house where such a gruesome murder was committed. Accordingly, one afternoon in early spring, I set off, walking stick in hand, for a stroll around that infamous residence.

I was evacuated to this rural farming village in Okayama Prefecture in May of last year, at the height of the bombing raids. And since that day, everyone I've met has talked to me at least once of what some call "the Koto Murder Case" and others "the Honjin Murder Case" at the home of the Ichiyanagi family.

Generally, as soon as people hear that I'm a writer of detective stories, they feel compelled to tell me of any murder case with which they have the slightest personal connection. I suppose rumours of my profession had reached the ears of the villagers, so every single one managed to bring up the topic of the Honjin Murder Case at some point. For the people of this village there could hardly be a more memorable case, and yet most of them were not aware of the full horror of this crime.

Usually when people tell me these kinds of tales, they never turn out to be as interesting to me as they are to the teller, much less potential material for a book. But this case was different. From the moment I heard the first whispers about the case, I was fascinated. Then, when I finally got to hear the account from the lips of F—, the man most directly connected to the case, I was at once seized with a great excitement. This was no ordinary murder. The perpetrator had scrupulously planned the whole ghastly deed. What's more, it was worthy of the label "Locked Room Murder Mystery".

The locked room murder mystery—a genre that any self-respecting detective novelist will attempt at some point in his or her career. The murder takes place in a room with no apparent way for the killer to enter or exit. Constructing a solution is an appealing challenge to the author. As my esteemed friend Eizo Inoue wrote, all of the works of the great John Dickson Carr are some variation on the locked room murder theme. As a writer of detective novels myself, I intended one day to try my hand at one of these, and now I've been unexpectedly blessed—one has fallen right into my lap. I know it's shocking but I feel I owe a debt of gratitude to the killer for devising such a fiendish method to stab this man and woman.

When I first heard the story, I immediately racked my brain to think of any similar cases among all the novels I've read. The first that came to mind were Gaston Leroux's *The Mystery of the Yellow Room* and Maurice Leblanc's *The Teeth of the Tiger;* then there's *The Canary Murder Case* and *The Kennel Murder Case*, both by S.S. Van Dine; and finally, Dickson Carr's *The Plague Court Murders.* I even considered that variation on the locked room murder theme of Roger Scarlett's *Murder Among the Angells.* But this real-life case wasn't quite like any of the above-mentioned. Maybe, just maybe, the killer had read a selection of stories like these, dissected all of the different devices used, then picked out the elements that he needed, constructing his own device… At least that's one theory.

10

Out of all of those books, it's *The Mystery of the Yellow Room* that bears the closest resemblance, at least as regards setting and atmosphere; less so, the facts of the case. In that story, the crime scene was a room with yellow wallpaper; in the Honjin Murder Case, the columns and beams, ceiling and rain shutters were all painted in red ochre. Red ochre wasn't an unusual hue for houses in this region—in fact, the house I was living in had also been painted that colour. The difference was that my house was extremely old, and the red lustre had faded to a dark brownish sheen. On the other hand, the room where the murder took place had just been repainted, and must have been gleaming with its fresh coat of red. The *tatami* mat flooring and the *fusuma* sliding doors that divided the two main rooms were brand new too, and there was a *byobu* folding screen decorated with gold leaf. The only unpleasant sight must have been the couple lying there, soaked in the crimson of their own blood.

To me, the most captivating element of this case was the way in which the traditional Japanese string instrument known as the *koto* was connected from beginning to end. At all the critical moments, its eerie music could be heard. I, who have never quite escaped the influences of romanticism, still find that incredibly alluring. A locked room murder, a red-ochre-painted room and the sound of the koto… all of these elements are so perfect—too perfect—like drugs that work a little too well. If I don't hurry to get it all down in writing, I fear their effects may start to wear off.

Now I seem to have got a little bit ahead of myself…

From my house to the grounds of the Ichiyanagi residence takes roughly fifteen minutes on foot. It's in the small hamlet of Yamanoya, just outside the larger village of O—.

11

A hill lies to the north of Yamanoya, made up of three gentle ridges, reminding me somehow of the legs of a starfish. At the very tip of one of those legs sits the grand residence of the Ichiyanagi family.

A small stream runs along the west side of the starfish hill, and on the east there is a narrow road coming from the village of H—. Shortly after the stream and the road round the foot of the hill, the two meet. The Ichiyanagi home occupies the roughly triangular acre and a half of land in between. In other words, the property is enclosed by the hill to the north, the stream to the west and the H— village road to the east. The main entrance faces the road on the east side.

I began by walking by that side with its grand black gate embellished with studs. An imposing wall stretched to both left and right, running for a total of about 350 feet. When I looked in through the gate, I saw that there was another inner fence, indicating that the property was as impressive as rumour had suggested. However, I couldn't see beyond this inner fence.

I tried walking around the south end of the premises to the west side, and then followed the stream in a northerly direction. At the very northern corner of the outer wall, I came across a broken-down waterwheel and a simple wooden bridge. I crossed the bridge and clambered up the steep side of the hill, ducking down to push my way through the thick bamboo that grew there. From up here on the hillside that formed the northern boundary of the Ichiyanagi property, I had almost a perfect bird's-eye view over the grounds.

The closest roof to me was that of the annexe house, the scene of that terrible murder. From what I'd heard in the village, this building had originally been constructed for the retired head of the Ichiyanagi family, and was much smaller than the main house, comprising only two rooms: one eight and the other six tatami mats in size. Yet typical of this type of structure, although the building itself was small, the garden was extensive, stretching both to the south and the west sides, and crammed with trees, bushes and ornamental rocks.

I'll write about this annexe house in more detail later. Looking beyond the annexe, further to the south, I could see the main building—the magnificent single-storey Ichiyanagi home, which faced in an easterly direction. And beyond that, the quarters occupied by the branch family. Next to this were the storehouse and several other small buildings dotted about, seemingly at random.

The main house and the annexe had been divided by a high fence and were connected by a means of a simple garden gate made of twigs and branches. Right now, the fence and gate were damaged almost beyond recognition, but at the time of the murder they were still in good shape, solid enough to slow down the people who came running at the sound of the screams.

This completed my survey of the Ichiyanagi residence, and I took a little while to scramble my way out of the bamboo thicket. Next, I headed back to O— local government office, right at the far south end of the village. There were few houses around that area, and further south again, nothing but rice fields until the next small town, K—. Running through those rice fields was a fairly major two-lane road. If you walked for about forty minutes total, you would come to N— train station. In other words, if you were travelling by train, there was no other way to enter O— village than by this road. You

13

were forced to pass in front of the government building on your way in.

Right across the street from it was a tavern with an earthen floor and a simple window in the front. It was a place where wagon drivers and other tradesmen would stop by for a quick drink and something to eat. But more significantly, the character who would go on to play a central role in what I'm calling the Honjin Murder Case made his first appearance at this very tavern. This was the first sighting of the three-fingered man…

The incident took place around sunset on 23rd November 1937, or the twelfth year of the reign of the Showa Emperor. In other words, two days before the murder.

The *okamisan*, proprietress of this tavern, was sitting on one of the wooden stools out front, gossiping with a couple of her regulars—a wagon driver and an official from the government office—as the figure of a man came hobbling down the road from the direction of K— town. When he reached the tavern, the man came to an abrupt halt.

"Could you tell me the way to the Ichiyanagi residence?"

The okamisan, the village official and the wagon driver stopped talking to look the man over. This wasn't the kind of person one would expect to visit the Ichiyanagi family. He wore a crumpled felt hat pulled low over his eyes and a large mask covered his nose and mouth. Matted hair poked out from under his hat, and there was stubble covering his face from cheek to jowl. All in all, he was a shady-looking character. He wasn't wearing a coat; the collar of his jacket was turned up against the cold, but that jacket and his trousers were smeared with grime and dust and worn away to a shine at the elbows and knees. His shoes were caked in grey dust and both soles were hanging off. Everything about the man looked run-down. It was hard to tell, but he was perhaps around thirty years old.

"The Ichiyanagi residence? It's that way. But what business do you have with the Ichiyanagi family?"

The village official glared at the man, who blinked repeatedly while mumbling something unintelligible behind his mask.

Just at that moment, on the same road from the very same direction that the man had come, a rickshaw appeared. The okamisan glanced at it, and turned back to the visitor.

"Hey, you! Look. Here's the very man you want to see, the master of the Ichiyanagi house."

The passenger in the rickshaw was a man of forty or so with a dark complexion and a severe expression on his face. He wore dark Western-style clothing, and sat stiffly upright in his seat. He never once glanced to the side, or took in his surroundings, but kept his eyes fixed on the road ahead. With his sharp cheekbones and prominent nose, there was something austere and unapproachable about him.

This was Kenzo, the current master of the house of Ichiyanagi. The rickshaw passed by in front of the group of onlookers and quickly disappeared around a bend in the road. The wagon driver waited until it was completely out of sight before turning to the okamisan.

"Rumour has it the master of the house has found himself a bride. Is that right?"

"Looks like it. The wedding's the day after tomorrow."

"Eh? Already? Now that's what I call quick."

"Well, if he wastes any more time, then someone might come up with new objections to the marriage. Now that it's been decided he's in a rush to get it done. He's quite a force of nature, that one, when he puts his mind to something."

"Well, I s'pose that'll be how he got to be such a big-shot scholar," said the village official. "Mind you, he did well to get the consent of the old matriarch."

"Well, of course *she* doesn't approve. But I heard she had to give in eventually. The more she opposed it, the more stubborn the young master became."

"How old is he now? About forty?" asked the wagon driver.

"Forty on the nose," replied the official. "And this is his first marriage."

"A middle-aged man in love. More passionate than a youngster, that's for sure."

"And the bride's only twenty-five or -six too," said the okamisan. "Rin-san's daughter, I heard. Landed herself a big fish. Now that's what I call marrying up!"

The official turned back to the okamisan. "Is she a stunner, then, the bride?"

"They say she's not all that good-looking. But she's a teacher at some girls' school, so she's clever and capable— I guess that makes her a good match for the master." The okamisan sighed. "Looks like all the young girls'll need an education from now on…"

"Okamisan, don't tell me you're planning to go to school to land yourself a rich husband?"

"Oh, you can bet I am."

The three of them burst out laughing. It was at that moment the strange visitor opened his mouth again.

"Okamisan," he said hesitantly, "could I possibly have a drink of water? My throat is so dry…"

Startled, the three friends turned. Truth be told, they'd completely forgotten that he was there. The okamisan scowled at him for a few moments, but eventually filled a glass with

16

water and handed it to him. The man thanked her, and shifted his mask so as to be able to drink. The three villagers exchanged a look.

There was a long gash on the man's right cheek that appeared to have been stitched up after an injury. It was a deep scar that ran from the right corner of his lip up his cheek, as if the side of his face had been slashed open. The reason the man was wearing a mask wasn't to protect him from dust or disease; it was to hide that scar. And there was one more gruesome detail that caught their eye. As he reached for the glass, they saw that he only had three fingers on his right hand. The ring finger and little finger were both cut in half; only the thumb and first two fingers were whole.

The three-fingered man finished his water, thanked the okamisan and hobbled off in the same direction the rickshaw had gone. The three locals were left staring after him.

"What the hell?…"

"What does he want with the Ichiyanagis?"

"Ugh, he gave me the creeps! Did you see that mouth? I'm never using that glass again!"

The okamisan placed the used glass on the very far end of the shelf, a decision which would prove to be helpful in the following days.

Incidentally, if you are the kind of reader who enjoys reading between the lines of a story, and recall the particulars of the crime, you may already be able to guess what I am about to write next. Namely, that you only need three fingers to play the koto. Its strings are traditionally plucked by the thumb, index and middle fingers.

CHAPTER 2

The Descendants of the Honjin

According to the village elders, the wealthy Ichiyanagi family wasn't originally from O— village at all, but from the neighbouring town of K—. This automatically made them unpopular among the narrow-minded villagers.

K— used to lie along the old Chugokukaido, a section of the main route linking east and west Japan. In the Edo Period it was a rest station for travellers, and the Ichiyanagi home was a *honjin*, or an inn where Edo Period nobility would stay. However, when the shogun was overthrown, and the imperial system was reinstated in the late 1860s, the family head realized that he was about to lose the honjin. He had the foresight to act before the old feudal system collapsed completely and moved his family to their current location. He was able to take advantage of the turmoil of the time and acquire farmland dirt cheap, instantly becoming a rich landowner. That was why the local folk liked to call the Ichiyanagi family a bunch of upstart *kappa*, mythical water goblins. This word was a local term of abuse for people who moved from K— town to O— village.

Anyway, at the time of the gruesome murder, the occupants of the Ichiyanagi family compound were as follows:

First and foremost, there was the widow of the previous head of the family, and mistress of the house, Itoko. She was at the time fifty-seven years old. She always wore her hair in a meticulously coiled chignon, and never once let her mask of dignity drop. Itoko was immensely proud of being a descendant of a honjin family. When the villagers spoke of the "old matriarch", this was to whom they referred.

The dowager Itoko had five children, but only three of them were living with her at the time. The oldest of these was her son Kenzo, a graduate of philosophy at a certain private university in Kyoto. He'd taught for a few years at his alma mater after graduation, but had fallen prey to a respiratory disorder and returned home, shutting himself away from the world. Nevertheless, he was a great scholar and being confined to the house didn't prevent him from dedicating himself to his studies. He wrote books, from time to time contributed articles to journals, and had become a well-known academic. Apparently it wasn't his poor health that had prevented him from marrying—he was just too busy with his studies to think about such matters.

After Kenzo came Itoko's elder daughter, Taeko. She had married a businessman and was living in Shanghai at the time, so had no direct connection to the events of that night. Itoko's second son, Ryuji, was thirty-five and a doctor, employed by a major hospital in Osaka. He had not been at the family home that night either. He rushed home right after hearing of the tragedy, and so had some involvement in the immediate aftermath.

For many years after giving birth to Ryuji, Itoko and her husband hadn't had any more children. Everyone thought there wouldn't be further additions to the family, but after a gap of almost ten years, she had another son, and then a full eight years after that, a daughter. The boy was called Saburo, and the girl Suzuko. At the time of the murder, Saburo was twenty-five, and Suzuko seventeen.

Saburo was definitely the black sheep of the family. He'd been expelled from middle school, and sent instead to a private vocational school in Kobe. He was expelled from that school too, and at the time of the murder had no occupation of any kind. He used to hang around the house all day. The consensus was that he was intelligent enough, but never applied himself to any kind of work. There was also a certain slyness to his nature. Down in the village he was pretty much universally despised.

As for the youngest child, Suzuko, well... I can't help feeling sorry for her. Perhaps it was because her parents were already quite old when they had her that she was rather delicate, like a flower that had to bloom in the shade. In addition to her poor physical health, she was a bit slow. She wasn't exactly mentally disabled—in some ways she was very gifted; in fact, when it came to playing the koto, one would go so far as to call her a musical genius. From time to time, she would show flashes of incredible insight, but in most everyday matters she behaved like a child of seven or eight.

These were the members of the main Ichiyanagi family, but there was another branch of the family living on the same property. The head of this branch family was Ryosuke, a cousin of Kenzo and his siblings. He was thirty-eight years old at the time, and he lived there with his wife, Akiko, and three young children. Obviously, these children had nothing to do with the murder case, and so I'll leave them off this list.

Ryosuke was completely different in temperament from his cousin Kenzo and the others. He'd only finished primary school, but being good at mathematics and a worldly type, he was the perfect person to manage the Ichiyanagi family's affairs. As far as Itoko was concerned, more than her eccentric oldest son, the absent second son and the untrustworthy third son, Ryosuke proved to be the closest to a confidant that she had in her life. As for his wife, Akiko, there was nothing particularly distinctive about her; she was just an ordinary woman, obedient to her husband.

And so these were the six inhabitants of the Ichiyanagi residence: Itoko the family matriarch, Kenzo, Saburo, Suzuko, Ryosuke and Akiko. Together they lived a conservative, traditional lifestyle, peaceful until the moment that Kenzo announced his engagement. Then it was as if a large pebble had been dropped into a still pond. The ripples spread wider and further, building into waves of anger. The woman Kenzo wanted to marry was Katsuko Kubo, a teacher at a girls' school in Okayama City. The Ichiyanagi family was united in their opposition to this marriage, not because they had any kind of problem with Katsuko personally, but because they objected to her lineage.

Gentle reader, the word "lineage", which has all but fallen out of usage in the city, is even today alive and well in rural villages like this one. You might even say it rules every aspect of people's lives. We are now in a period of upheaval following the Second World War, and farmers and peasants are increasingly no longer obliged to kowtow to the upper classes, or to show the same level of respect for those with high social standing, fortune or property. Those values have come crashing down in the wake of Japan's defeat.

However, what is still intact is lineage. The reverence, respect and pride associated with being born into a family with distinguished ancestry are still alive and well in rural communities. And lineage has nothing whatsoever to do with genetics or eugenics. For example, if the family of an established community leader, such as someone who'd been a village headman in the days of the shogunate, started producing male children who suffered from physical disabilities or epilepsy or lunacy, each would still be permitted to serve as headman when his time came because his family line was good. This is still true now, and even more so in 1937, when this story takes place. As far as the Ichiyanagi family was concerned, there was nothing in the world more important than being the descendants of the owners of a honjin. It was everything to them.

Katsuko Kubo's father had once been a tenant farmer in O— village. But he'd been rather more ambitious than the average peasant. He had left the village, along with his younger brother, and set sail for America. There the brothers had found work on fruit farms until they had saved enough money to return to Japan and establish their own orchard about twenty-five miles from their home village. Both brothers married, but the elder died shortly after his wife had given birth to their daughter, Katsuko. Upon the death of her husband, the young widow had returned to her home village, leaving Katsuko to be raised by her uncle. She turned out to be a very studious child, and her uncle spared no expense in paying her school tuition. After graduating from a teacher-training school in Tokyo, she took a job in a girls' school in Okayama City, not too far from her home.

The fruit farm established by Katsuko's father and uncle was hugely successful. Katsuko's uncle was scrupulously honest when it came to putting his niece's share aside for her, so that she worked as a schoolteacher not because it was necessary to make a living, but because it was what she wanted to do. She was a woman in possession of both her own fortune and a career.

Despite this, in the eyes of the Ichiyanagi family, it didn't matter how educated she was, how wise or intelligent, or how large a fortune she possessed—the daughter of a tenant farmer would always be just that: the daughter of a tenant farmer. She had no family name, no pedigree, and they thought of her as no more than the child of Rinkichi Kubo, poor peasant farmer.

Kenzo had met Katsuko when he'd been invited to speak at a students' group in Kurashiki City. Katsuko was a member of the group. After this initial meeting, Katsuko used to visit Kenzo to ask him for help with the foreign-language books she liked to read. This relationship continued for about a year, until suddenly one day Kenzo proposed marriage.

I've already mentioned how the Ichiyanagi family opposed this marriage, led by Itoko and Kenzo's cousin Ryosuke. Out of Kenzo's own siblings, it was his sister Taeko who felt the most strongly about the engagement; she even wrote a vehement letter to her older brother on the subject. On the other hand, the middle brother, Ryuji, supported Kenzo and privately sent a letter to Itoko saying that she should let her eldest son do as he liked. However, he never said a word about this directly to his older brother.

And what was Kenzo's reaction to all this criticism? His approach was to stay completely silent. He made no move whatsoever to respond to any of it. And of course, water eventually wins over fire. One by one, the opponents ran out of heat, their voices faded, their steps faltered and finally, with a wry smile and a shoulder shrug, they were forced to admit defeat.

The wedding ceremony was held on 25th November 1937. And that very night, the heinous crime was committed. However, before I can get to the gory details of the murder, I must mention a few apparently trivial incidents that seem to have been some kind of prelude to what finally transpired.

These all took place on the day before the wedding; in other words, on 24th November in the afternoon. The scene was the Ichiyanagi family sitting room, where Itoko and Kenzo were taking tea, and having what was clearly an uncomfortable conversation. The youngest, Suzuko, was sitting nearby, happily playing with a doll. This was typical of Suzuko—wherever she went she was absorbed in her own world and never got in anyone's way.

"But that has been the tradition in this house for generations."

Itoko had already lost to her son over his choice of marriage partner, and was apparently still unable to hide her displeasure.

"But, Mother, we didn't do that when Ryuji got married."

Kenzo didn't even deign to glance at the sweet *manju* bun offered to him by his mother. Instead, with a sour face, he continued to smoke his cigarette.

"That's because he's the second son. You and Ryuji aren't the same at all. You are the heir of this family, and Katsuko-san will be the wife of the heir."

"But I don't think Katsuko can even play the koto. She can probably play the piano."

That was the topic of their quarrel. For several generations, the bride of the heir to the family title had been expected to play certain pieces on a koto at the official wedding ceremony.

"So you see, Mother, there's no point in bringing this up now," Kenzo went on. "If you'd told me about this earlier, I could have prepared Katsuko."

"My intention isn't to put any kind of damper on the wedding ceremony. I don't want you to think that I'm trying to embarrass Katsuko in any way. However, family tradition is what it is…"

Just as the tension in the room was beginning to mount, Suzuko came to the rescue.

"Mama, can't I play the koto?"

Itoko was taken by surprise, but Kenzo gave a wry smile.

"That's a lovely idea. Thank you, Suzuko. Mother, surely no one could object to Suzuko's playing?"

Itoko seemed about to concede, but right at that moment her nephew, Ryosuke, appeared in the sitting room and addressed his young cousin.

"Suzu-chan! This is where you've been hiding. I've been looking for you everywhere. See, I've finished making that box for you!"

He was holding a beautifully fashioned wooden box of the size that usually held *mikan*—mandarin oranges. Itoko frowned:

"Ryo-san, what's that?"

"It's Tama's coffin. Suzu-chan was upset when someone said she should bury him in a mikan box. She said, 'Poor Tama being stuck in an old box like that.' She refused to use it, so I managed to make this one instead."

"Yes, poor Tama!" Suzuko echoed. "Thank you, Ryosuke."

Tama was the name of Suzuko's pet kitten, but for the past few days it had suffered from vomiting and diarrhoea, and had finally died that morning.

25

Itoko grimaced slightly at the sight of this wooden coffin.

"Ryo-san," she said quickly, as if to change the subject, "what do you think of Suzuko being the one to play the koto?"

"Sounds all right to me, Aunt Itoko," said Ryosuke lightly, helping himself to a manju bun. Kenzo kept his back turned to his cousin and continued to puff on his cigarette.

At which point Saburo came in.

"Hey, Suzu-chan, that's a pretty box you've got there! Who made that for you?"

"You're mean, Sabu-chan. You lied to me—you promised to make one for me, but you didn't. Anyway, Cousin Ryosuke made this for me so I don't need yours any more."

"Really, Suzu-chan. I can't believe you still don't trust me!"

"Saburo, did you get a haircut?" said Itoko, glancing at her son's head.

"Yes, just now. By the way, Mother, I just heard something very strange at the barber's."

Itoko didn't respond, so Saburo turned instead to his elder brother.

"Kenzo, yesterday evening you went by the O— government office in a rickshaw, right? Did you happen to notice a weird-looking character hanging around outside the tavern?"

Kenzo looked puzzled.

"What do you mean by a weird character, Sabu-chan?" Ryosuke asked, his mouth stuffed full of manju.

"Well, it's really creepy. They say he had a huge scar from his mouth up his cheek like this. And then he had only three fingers on his right hand, just his thumb and the next two fingers… Anyway, it seems this man was asking the okamisan about our house. Hey, Suzuko, you didn't notice any strange men hanging around yesterday evening, did you?"

Suzuko looked up at Saburo and began to mumble, *Thumb, index finger, middle finger.* As she did so, she moved each of the corresponding fingers on her right hand as if playing the koto.

Itoko and Saburo watched her in silence. Ryosuke was busy peeling the paper off another manju. Kenzo kept on smoking his cigarette.

CHAPTER 3

The Sound of a Koto

As I said before, a honjin was a kind of inn in feudal Japan where *daimyo* lords and other important officials would stay on their way to or from paying attendance on the Shogun in the capital, Edo—the old name for Tokyo. Ordinary members of the public were not permitted to stay at a honjin. A family who owned such a high-class lodging house were also members of the elite, and so it followed that this was a place where the rules of high society were closely adhered to. There were differences between a honjin in this region and one on the Tokaido route, closer to Edo. First of all, there were fewer daimyo travelling on the Chugokukaido, and accordingly there were variations in the scale of operations, but a honjin was still a honjin.

In keeping with the honour associated with being descendants of a honjin family, the wedding celebrations of the current head of the Ichiyanagi clan were expected to be a flamboyant affair. The following report was made to me by F— who was kind enough to offer me an insight into the usual customs of the region:

"These kinds of events are way more grandiose in the countryside than they are in the city. And with a family as important as the Ichiyanagis, and the groom being the heir to the family line, he would be dressed in a *kamishimo*, the formal dress of the samurai; the bride would wear a white kimono with an *uchikake* robe over it. Normally there would be between fifty and a hundred guests."

But this particular wedding turned out to be an extremely private gathering. On the bridegroom's side, besides the immediate family members, there was only a great-uncle from K— town in attendance. Kenzo's own brother, Ryuji, didn't even come back from Osaka. The only person to attend from the bride's side was her uncle, Ginzo Kubo.

Consequently, the ceremony itself was a rather forlorn affair, but there was no question of skimping on the celebrations for the many tenant farmers and farmhands who lived and worked on the Ichiyanagi land. It was tradition in these parts for the newly-weds to drink all night with the locals.

And so, on the day of the wedding ceremony, 25th November, the kitchen at the Ichiyanagi residence was bustling, with extra hands drafted in to help alongside the usual servants. Around 6.30 p.m., when preparations were at their busiest, a man suddenly appeared at the kitchen door.

"Excuse me, is the master home? Would somebody mind passing this to him?"

Old Nao turned from lighting the fire under a pot to see a man wearing a crumpled felt hat pulled down low over his eyes, the collar of his worn old jacket turned up against the cold and an oversized mask hiding most of his face. A very suspicious-looking character, she thought.

"You want to see the master of the house?"

"Um… yes. I need to give this to him."

In his left hand, the man was holding a scrap of paper, folded over several times. Later, when interviewed by the police, Nao would describe his appearance this way:

"It was weird. He had all his fingers curled around it. He was clutching the paper between the knuckles of his forefinger and middle finger. Like a leper would… Yes, that's right, he kept his right hand in his pocket. I thought there was something off about him, so I tried to get a good look at his face, but he quickly turned his head away. Then he shoved the paper at me and ran away, right out the kitchen door."

There were lots of other people in the kitchen at the time, but nobody could have dreamed how significant the man's visit would turn out to be, and so nobody paid him any attention.

After the man ran off, the servant stood there for a while with the paper in her hand, not quite sure what to do until Ryosuke's wife, Akiko, hurried into the kitchen.

"Does anyone know where my husband's got to?"

"I think he just went out."

"Hmm. I wonder what's so urgent when we're this busy? Never mind. If you see him, please tell him he needs to get changed as soon as possible."

Nao called to Akiko to wait and handed her the piece of paper, explaining what had just happened. On closer inspection it looked like a page torn from a pocket diary.

"For Kenzo-san? I see…"

Akiko frowned slightly, but didn't slow her pace. Tucking the paper into the *obi* sash of her kimono, she left the kitchen and peered into the sitting room. Itoko was in there in conversation with her maid, Kiyo, who was helping her with her formal kimono. Suzuko, already wearing her own kimono, sat by her mother's side, plucking at a beautiful gold-lacquered koto.

"Auntie, where's Kenzo-san?"

"I don't know. He's probably in his study. Just a moment, Akiko-san, would you help Kiyo tie my obi?"

Right as Akiko and the maid had finished tying Itoko's obi sash, Saburo came ambling in wearing a heavy winter kimono.

"Saburo, why are you still in those clothes?... Where have you been?"

"I was in the study."

"Reading another of those detective books, I'll bet," Suzuko said, as she tuned the koto. Saburo was obsessed with mystery novels.

"What's wrong with reading novels? How about you, Suzuko? Have you held a funeral for that cat yet?"

Suzuko ignored him and kept playing.

"If you haven't then you'd better hurry up. If you leave a dead cat lying around, it's going to turn into a howling ghost."

Suzuko looked upset.

"You can be as mean as you like, Sabu-chan, but I already did Tama-chan's funeral this morning."

"Stop it, Saburo! That's completely inappropriate," Itoko admonished him. "Be careful what you say. By the way, was your brother in the study?"

"No. Isn't he in the annexe?"

"Akiko-san, if you find Kenzo could you tell him to start getting ready as soon as possible? The bride will be arriving any time now."

Akiko left the sitting room and just as she started to slip on her *geta* garden sandals to head over to the annexe house, her husband, Ryosuke, came strolling casually out of the branch family house, still in his everyday clothes.

"What are you thinking? You need to start getting dressed or you won't be ready in time!"

"Don't be ridiculous. The bride won't be here until eight. There's no hurry. And anyway, where are you off to?"

"To the annexe to look for Kenzo-san…"

Kenzo was standing on the wooden *engawa* veranda of the annexe house, staring up at the sky.

"Aki-san," he said, as he saw her heading his way, "it looks as if the weather's going to change. What? This is for me?… Ah, thanks."

Kenzo took the note from Akiko and moved inside to read it under the electric light. Akiko followed and began to adjust the flower arrangement in the *tokonoma* alcove.

"Aki-san, tell me who brought you this note!"

Noticing something out of the ordinary in Kenzo's tone of voice, Akiko stopped and turned to look at him. Kenzo was standing over her with a look of animal fury on his face.

"I… er… Nao-san was the one who gave it to me. She said it was delivered by a kind of vagrant. Is there some problem or…"

Kenzo continued to glare at Akiko as she spoke, but then he seemed to remember himself and turned away. His eye fell on the note again. He grabbed it, ripped it into shreds, then looked around for some place to dispose of the pieces. Finding nowhere appropriate, he stuffed them into the sleeve of his kimono.

"Kenzo-san, your mother asked me to tell you to prepare for the ceremony."

"Yes, right. Aki-san, would you mind closing the shutters?"

And with that, Kenzo left the annexe house.

The previous all happened around seven in the evening. About an hour later the bride arrived, accompanied by the official matchmakers, and the wedding ceremony began.

32

As I previously mentioned, there were very few wedding guests. On the groom's side the dowager Itoko; brother and sister Saburo and Suzuko; the branch family husband and wife, Ryosuke and Akiko; and one more, a seventy-year-old great-uncle from K— town by the name of Ihei. The sole guest on the bride's side was her uncle, Ginzo Kubo. The official matchmaker was the mayor of the village, but this was a mere formality; he was just there for show.

After the pledges were made and sake cups exchanged, the beautiful black- and gold-embellished koto was brought out, and Suzuko performed as had been arranged. Suzuko may have been backward for her age in most regards, but when it came to the koto she was incredibly accomplished. The player and the instrument together filled that room with their beauty.

However, a koto performance during a wedding ceremony was very unusual, and the piece that Suzuko played was one that Katsuko had never heard before, so the bride was rather confused. Itoko explained it to her:

"Many years ago, the wife of the head of the Ichiyanagi family was a very talented koto player. It so happened that a noblewoman—the daughter of a daimyo—was passing through on her way west for a wedding ceremony and stopped at the honjin. The expert koto player performed a song that she had written herself called 'The Lovebirds'. The daimyo's daughter admired the song so much that the next day she sent the family a koto, which they nicknamed 'The Lovebird'. Ever since, the Ichiyanagi family has required the bride of the heir to play the koto at her wedding ceremony. The piece that Suzuko just played was 'The Lovebirds' and the instrument that she used was that very same Lovebird koto."

Hearing this, Katsuko's eyes grew wide.

"So I should have been playing the koto just now?"

"That's right. But as I had no idea whether you were aware of our tradition or not, I hesitated to ask, and requested Suzuko to play in your place."

Katsuko refrained from responding. Instead Ginzo Kubo answered for his niece.

"If Katsuko had been asked beforehand, she would gladly have played for you."

"Really? Big sister, do you play the koto too?" asked Suzuko.

"Miss, this young lady is going to become a good companion to you," said Ginzo, addressing Suzuko. "And perhaps she'll be more than just your big sister. She could be your koto teacher too."

Itoko and Ryosuke exchanged glances. Seeing this, Kenzo spoke up.

"So then this koto belongs to Katsuko now."

Itoko didn't respond right away, and there was an awkward silence in the room. It was the worldly-wise mayor who came to the rescue:

"If the bride is talented at the koto, she really ought to have been invited to play today." He turned to Itoko. "There's still the final part of the ceremony to take place in the annexe building. What do you think, madam, about a second performance?"

"That's true," said Itoko. "Would you play for us, Katsuko-san? As we've already had Suzuko perform 'The Lovebirds', please choose any piece. Something joyful that you like to play… It is after all this family's tradition for the bride to play the koto on her wedding night."

And that was how it came about that Katsuko played the koto later that evening.

The wedding ceremony ended around 9.30 p.m. and that was when the drinking and merrymaking began for guests in the house and kitchen alike.

Before they finally get to retire on their wedding night, all newly-weds have to go through something of an ordeal, but in the countryside it's especially tough. Kenzo and Katsuko were obliged to bring sake to their guests long into the dead of night.

As they served the locals in the kitchen, they were treated to lewd songs. Back in the house of course they weren't subjected to anything so bad, but Great-Uncle Ihei got blind drunk and starting ranting incoherently.

This character was the younger brother of Kenzo and Ryosuke's grandfather, but he had set up his own branch of the family when he was young, and they referred to him as the sub-branch uncle. Like most elderly men he was known for being quarrelsome and fond of his drink. On top of that he had all kinds of objections to and complaints about the wedding, and the more he drank the worse he got, spewing out his disgust directly to the bride and groom. Finally they entreated him to stay over, as he was in no state to make it home safely, but he refused to listen. Eventually, after midnight, he announced he was leaving.

"Saburo, you'd better see him home."

Kenzo, who'd done a good job of ignoring Ihei's abusive language, was kind enough to be worried about the drunken old man getting home in the dark.

"And as it's so late you might as well stay over at Uncle's place too."

It wasn't until they opened the door for Ihei to leave that they all realized it was snowing, and rather heavily too. It was rare for snow to fall at all in those parts, and to see it really piling up, it was natural that everyone was surprised. When they recalled events later, they would realize the crucial role that this snow had played in the terrible crime that was about to be committed.

Finally the newly-weds were able to retire to the annexe, and it was about one in the morning when they performed the last of the ritual exchanges of sake cups. In the words of Ryosuke's wife, Akiko, this is what happened:

"I carried the koto to the annexe with the help of the maid, Kiyo. They performed the sake ceremony, but the only family members present were Aunt Itoko, my husband and myself. Sabu-chan had gone to take Uncle Ihei home and Suzu-chan had already gone to bed. After the ceremony, Katsuko played 'Chidori' for us. When she'd finished, we leaned the koto vertically up against the tokonoma alcove. I placed the box of picks in the far corner of the alcove, but I don't really remember clearly whether the *katana* was on the shelf at that time."

It was almost two in the morning by the time the ceremonies were finished. The family left the newly-weds alone in the annexe and went back to the main house. At that time, it was still snowing heavily.

Then, some two hours later, a blood-curdling scream rang out, followed by the eerie strains of a koto being plucked with wild abandon.

CHAPTER 4

A Great Tragedy

Ginzo Kubo lay down in the spare room of the Ichiyanagi home where he was to spend the night. He suddenly felt very weary. This wasn't surprising. He had his own misgivings about his niece's marriage.

He knew all too well the feudal manners and sentiments of a rural village, and what this might mean for a lower-born woman such as Katsuko. If he was honest about it, he was concerned about how she might be treated. He wasn't convinced that joining the Ichiyanagi family—his former landlords—would bring Katsuko happiness.

But Katsuko herself had been eager to marry Kenzo. Ginzo's wife had offered her own view:

"I'm sure if your brother had been alive, he would have been thrilled about it. Marrying into the Ichiyanagi family is a huge mark of success."

Ginzo had let himself be convinced. His older brother, Rinkichi, had a far deeper admiration of Japanese traditions and class structure than Ginzo ever did. It was true—if Rinkichi had been alive, he would have been very proud of his daughter's match. In the end, despite his misgivings, Ginzo had given his consent to the marriage.

Once he'd made his decision, he rushed full speed ahead. So as not to embarrass Katsuko, he made sure there was nothing the Ichiyanagis could grumble about behind her back. He threw himself into organizing the wedding with the greatest efficiency. He drew on everything he had learned during his stay in America and ordered wedding clothes from the finest tailors in Kyoto and Osaka. He spared no expense.

"Uncle Ginzo, I can't believe you've spent so much on me!"

Katsuko was so taken aback at the lavish kimonos he'd bought for her that she burst into tears. But in the end all of Ginzo's efforts would be in vain...

That evening, Katsuko had set out from the house of the village mayor, who was invited to act as the go-between for the wedding. Decked out in her formal wedding kimono, her beauty left a great impression on everyone who saw her. The magnificence of the furniture and dishes and decorative items that had been sent as a dowry were the talk of the whole village. Ginzo was pleased to see that even the haughty Ichiyanagis were impressed.

"Rinkichi would have been gratified to see this," he said to himself that night, after the wedding was over. "He would have been truly delighted."

And with that, he felt his heart swell and tears begin to trickle down his cheek.

The sound of bawdy songs drifted over from the kitchen where the locals were still drinking. He tossed and turned, unable to fall asleep with all the racket, but eventually he drifted off.

Some time later he was woken from a fitful and dream-filled sleep. His eyes snapped open—had he just heard a scream?

He sat up in his futon. It wasn't a dream. He heard the same sound again—he couldn't tell if it was a man or a woman. Over and over it came—one voice, two voices, again and again, screams that were so terrifying they seemed to tear through the stillness of the night. Then from somewhere nearby, he heard the sound of hurried footsteps on a wooden floor.

The annexe house! Those screams came from the annexe! Instantly, Ginzo was pulling on his shirt and a gown over his pyjamas. He checked his watch: 4.15 a.m.

And that was when he heard the koto.

Pling pling thrum thrummm—the sound of all thirteen strings of the instrument being quickly plucked, followed right away by a loud *thump* like a folding screen falling over. And then dead silence. The merrymaking in the kitchen appeared to be over.

Ginzo slid open the shutters of his room. The snow had already stopped; a sliver of moon glinted coldly in the night sky. The garden was coated in a thick, downy layer of snow.

A figure appeared, struggling through the snow.

"Who's that?" Ginzo challenged the shadow.

"Ah, hello, sir. Did you hear that too?"

It was a male servant whom Ginzo had never seen before.

"Yes, I heard it. What on earth was it? Wait a moment. I'll go with you."

Throwing on his overcoat, Ginzo stepped into the outdoor geta by the door and out into the snow. As he moved across the garden, there was the sound of *amado* rain shutters being opened here and there. Itoko appeared at the door of the main house.

"Is that you out there, Genshichi? What was that voice I just heard?"

"Mama, I heard a koto." Suzuko's face appeared under her mother's sleeve.

"I don't know what it could have been," replied the servant, shivering. "It sounded like somebody crying for help."

Ginzo made straight for the gate in the fence that divided the main house from the annexe, and at that moment from the direction of the branch family's house on the far south edge of the compound, Ryosuke appeared, fumbling with his obi sash as he ran.

"Aunt Itoko, what was that noise?"

"Ah, Ryo-chan, could you check the annexe for me?"

Ginzo was pulling and rattling the tall garden gate. It seemed to be bolted on the opposite side and he couldn't get it open. Ryosuke threw himself shoulder first at the gate several times over, but although it was only made of branches and twigs, and appeared frail and rickety, the gate proved unexpectedly sturdy.

"Genshichi, go fetch an axe!"

"Yes, sir!"

Just as Genshichi turned to go, once more from the direction of the annexe house came the sound of a koto.

Ping ping ping, like the sound of each koto string being played in turn, then a loud *twang, zing, zing* vibrated through the air. It sounded as if a string had snapped.

"What was that?" said the servant, stopping in his tracks.

The moonlight reflecting off the snow revealed a whole collection of pale faces.

"Genshichi, why are you wasting time?" barked Ryosuke. "Go and get that axe!"

By the time the servant returned with the axe, Itoko and Suzuko, along with several maids and other male servants, were gathered around the gate. Ryosuke's wife, Akiko, arrived a little after the others, but she had thought to bring a lantern.

Genshichi swung the axe and after a few blows the gate came off its hinges and fell inwards. Ryosuke made to go through first, but for some reason Ginzo grabbed him by the shoulder and pulled him back. Then he stood for a few moments in front of the garden gate, taking in the annexe house and its surroundings.

"No footprints anywhere," he muttered, and looked back over his shoulder.

"Everyone, wait there! You two come with me."

Ginzo indicated Ryosuke and the servant, Genshichi.

"Take care... Make sure you don't kick up the snow too much. Akiko-san, would you mind lending me that lantern?"

Social rank and class mean nothing in an emergency. Everyone present was overwhelmed by Ginzo's unexpected leadership skills, and not a single person protested. Only Ryosuke seemed to be having trouble concealing his annoyance at having to take orders from this upstart tenant farmer. If he had only realized that this was a man who had succeeded in putting himself through college in America, he would surely have shown him some respect.

As they passed through the garden gate, there was another low bamboo fence running on their left side along the path to the front door of the building. But, looking over it into the annexe garden, they saw that the cotton-wool snow was completely untouched.

There seemed to be lights on in the building: an electric glow spilled out from the decorative *ranma* transoms at the top of the amado rain shutters.

The entrance to the annexe house was at its east end, and that was where the three men headed first. However, they found that the red-ochre-painted lattice door and the solid

41

wooden door beyond were both locked. They could see a key in the inside lock of the lattice door. They pushed and pulled on this door, but it wouldn't budge. Ryosuke and Genshichi banged as hard as they could on the slats, and called Kenzo's name at the top of their lungs, but there was no reply.

Ginzo's expression hardened. He left the front entrance, stepped over the low fence and walked around the south side of the building. The other two followed. The painted amado were tightly closed on this side. Ryosuke and Genshichi took it in turns to bang on the shutters and shout Kenzo's name, but still there was no response.

The three men made their way further around the building to the west side, continuing to bang on the shutters. Ryosuke suddenly stopped in his tracks. A kind of strangled noise came from deep in his throat.

"What's the matter?"

Ryosuke raised a finger and pointed. He was visibly trembling.

"Tha… That!"

Ginzo and Genshichi followed his gaze. What they saw made them gasp. About six feet away from the west end of the annexe house stood a tall stone lantern. Near its base, stuck blade-first into the snow, was a katana. Genshichi's immediate reaction was to run towards it, but once again Ginzo had the foresight to stop him.

"Don't touch it!"

Ginzo raised his lantern and looked around the dark thicket of bushes that surrounded them, but nowhere could he see a single footprint. Meanwhile Ryosuke went to investigate the rain shutters, but they were all properly closed and locked. They didn't appear to have been disturbed in any way.

"Sir, shall I try to look in through the ranma up there?"

Genshichi indicated the decorative panel above the west-side shutters.

"Yes, give it a try."

In the north-west corner, the lavatory area protruded from the rest of the building. In the bit of garden between this extension and the box that would hold the horizontally sliding rain shutters when they were open, there was a decorative stone basin. Genshichi climbed onto this basin and peered into the room through the transom.

Now this particular transom will come up again, so I will give a simple explanation of it right now. In traditional Japanese houses, the ranma is a wooden panel with openwork carving, situated above the wooden sliding amado, or rain shutters, and the *shoji* sliding paper doors. Its purpose is to let light and air into the room when the rain shutters and/ or the interior shoji doors are closed. The one at the west end of the annexe building was rather simple: a thick tree branch laid horizontally. It was uncarved and hadn't been sawn into a flat plank. It had been left in its natural form, with even the bark intact, the beauty in its natural curves. Here and there it had been planed away slightly, so that it would rest against the door lintel below and the cross-beam above, but in other places, due to the natural curvature of the branch there was quite a gap where light and air could enter. That said, none of the gaps was over five inches at most—definitely not enough space for a person to climb in or out. The lintel and the cross-beam and the shutters around it were all painted red ochre, as I mentioned at the beginning of this story.

Genshichi peered through this ranma.

"One of the shoji doors at this end of the room is open. Then the shoji by the tokonoma is slightly open too… And the byobu screen has fallen over this way, but I can't see anything beyond that. Nothing in the tatami part."

The three men began again to call Kenzo's and Katsuko's names, but still there was nothing.

"We'll have to break the shutters."

The rain shutters were locked together all the way around the house, and there was no way to remove just one of them. Genshichi rushed off to retrieve the axe he'd left by the garden gate. As Ryosuke and Ginzo were waiting for him to return, they suddenly heard the sound of somebody up on the cliff behind them. They hurried to the corner by the lavatory extension.

"Who is it?" demanded Ryosuke. "Who's up there?"

Right in front of them there was a towering camphor tree that blocked their view, but then from the bamboo thicket above came a voice.

"Is that the master of the branch family speaking?"

"Oh, it's Sho-san. What are you doing up there?"

"I heard a strange noise so I ran out to look. And then I heard your voice, sir."

"Who's this Sho-san?" asked Ginzo.

"What? Oh, it's the man in charge of the mill that polishes the rice. He comes to run the waterwheel. It's Shokichi, one of our servants."

I believe at the opening of this book I mentioned a broken-down waterwheel on the stream that ran along the west side of the Ichiyanagi property. Well, at the time of the story, the mill was still in operation, and Shokichi would come early every morning to hull and polish the rice. As you will discover later, this would prove crucial to the mystery.

"Shokichi-san, you say that you ran out of the mill the moment you heard the voices. Is that right?" asked Ginzo. "Did you by any chance happen to see any suspicious characters?"

"No. Not a soul. I heard the voices, came out of the mill and stopped for a bit back there on the bridge. That's when I heard the koto the second time. That kind of *ping ping* and then the twanging noise. I climbed up and ran along the edge of the cliff, but I didn't see a thing."

That was when Genshichi returned with the axe. Ginzo asked Shokichi to keep an eye open for anything untoward and went back to the west side of the house. At Ryosuke's orders, Genshichi swung the axe at one of the rain shutters. With the first blow a crack appeared in the wood large enough for Ryosuke to reach inside and slide the wooden bolt that locked it shut. He slid the shutter to the side.

The three men dashed in through the open space, crossed the engawa, the corridor running around the house, but were brought to a halt by the sight that met them in the room beyond. It was a scene of carnage.

Kenzo and Katsuko lay slashed and soaked in blood. The futon with its decorated cover, the freshly replaced tatami-mat flooring and even the gilded folding screen that had been knocked over, were all bloody. What had happened to the heavenly dream that was supposed to be their wedding night? All that was left was a tableau from hell.

Genshichi almost collapsed in shock but Ginzo caught him by the shoulder and steered him out of the room.

"Call a doctor and the police. Then make sure no one comes through that gate."

After Genshichi ran off, Ginzo stared for a while at the

two bodies, a look of fury on his face. Then he began to look around the tatami room.

The first thing he noticed was the koto. The black koto with its gold lacquer embellishments was by Katsuko's side. As if someone with bloody fingers had been playing the instrument, twelve of its strings, right at the point where the musician would pluck them, were adorned with a streak of blood. The thirteenth string had been snapped right in the middle and both ends had curled up on themselves. The bridge that had supported the broken string was missing.

The string had snapped and the bridge was missing...

Next it occurred to Ginzo to check the locks on all the doors and windows. All the rain shutters, including those by the front entranceway, were undisturbed. One by one, he opened the doors to the *oshiire* closet in the smaller tatami-mat room, the lavatory area on the west side and the little storage closet opposite the toilet, and checked inside each one. At the end of the bit of corridor in front of the toilet was a small window, but there was no sign that anyone had opened it.

Returning to the main tatami room, he found Ryosuke still standing there as if frozen.

"I don't understand it," Ginzo told him. "It's a mystery. There's nobody hiding in here anywhere. And there's nowhere anyone could have got out. Maybe..."

Maybe?... Ryosuke caught Ginzo's meaning right away and shook his head furiously.

"It's not possible. There is no way it could be suicide. Look at that screen."

Ginzo followed Ryosuke's gaze, and saw on the upturned side of the fallen byobu screen a bloody handprint, the blood still wet. Strangely, there were only three fingerprints—the thumb, index finger and middle finger. But there was something else that was truly bizarre about this three-fingered handprint...

CHAPTER 5

A New Use for a Koto Pick

The father of F—, the man who provided me with the background information for my story, used to be the village doctor. He is now sadly departed, but the morning after the murder it was Doctor F— who was the first to arrive on the scene.

The doctor appears to have been fascinated by the Honjin Murder Case, and made detailed notes which I am still able to consult today. Much of this story has been recreated from the content of those notes. Among them was a sketch of the scene in and around the annexe house. When writing a book of this kind, such materials are extremely helpful for keeping track of what occurred, so I'm going to include the manuscript sketch.

It was about six o'clock and the sun was starting to come up by the time Doctor F— and the local police constable arrived. As soon as the constable saw the scene of the crime, he called the main police station in S— town to report a major incident. The S— town police station in turn called the prefectural police headquarters, so police investigators kept turning up, each more senior than the last. The location was so remote that it was reportedly already noon by the time everyone was assembled.

The investigators must have conducted a crime-scene investigation and interviewed everyone connected to the victims, but it surely isn't necessary to cover all that in detail

PLAN OF THE ICHIYANAGI ANNEXE HOUSE

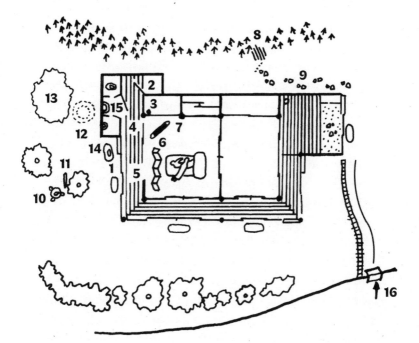

KEY

1. rain shutter broken by Ryosuke, Genshichi, and Ginzo

2. storage closet where the killer hid

3. box of koto picks in tokonoma alcove

4. shoji screen, slightly open

5. shoji screen, fully open

6. byobu folding screen, fallen

7. koto

8. marks left where the killer apparently slid down the cliffside

9. footprints

10. stone lantern

11. katana stuck in the snow

12. pile of fallen leaves

13. camphor tree

14. stone basin

15. lavatory area

16. garden gate

here. I really don't want to bore my readers, so I will just summarize for you the findings of the chief investigator, Detective Inspector Isokawa.

First, there was the problem of the footprints. Inspector Isokawa arrived around eleven that morning, but by then the snow had already begun to melt. There was no reason to doubt Ginzo's, Ryosuke's and the servant Genshichi's testimonies that there hadn't been a single footprint in the snow. This information caused the inspector great anxiety, but in fact it wasn't quite true that there were no footprints whatsoever.

I invite you to take another look at the sketch of the annexe house. There's a steep hillside, or a kind of cliff edge, to the north of the building. Between this cliff and the annexe there's a strip of empty land about six feet wide. The clifftop is thick with bamboo trees that hang out over the edge with the result that the snow didn't pile up directly below the cliff that night. It was in this empty area close to the east end of the annexe that there were some visible muddy footprints. And not only footprints—according to the police there were also signs that somebody had slid down the side of the cliff into the grounds. As you can see on the sketch, the footprints head towards the east entrance to the building, but once they get close they disappear, presumably because they were covered by a layer of snow. But then, on the earthen floor of the *genkan* entranceway, where shoes are removed before stepping up into the house, there were two more muddy footprints that appeared to be identical to the others. In summary, whoever had slid down the side of the cliff had then walked east and entered the annexe house by its front door.

Those footprints were strangely misshapen—there was an extremely deep impression at the toe, and a much lighter, twisted one at the heel. It was clear to anyone that they had been made by a pair of old, worn-out shoes. There was nobody in the Ichiyanagi household who owned a pair of shoes like that; thus it was reasonable to assume that the footprints belonged to the murderer. In other words, the murderer had come sliding down the cliff behind the annexe house and had crept in through the main entrance. But what time could this have happened?… Well, the snow was very useful in working this out.

The snow had started falling around nine o'clock the previous evening, and had stopped at around three in the morning. This meant that the murderer had snuck into the house before nine, or at least before it began to snow heavily around 2 a.m. However, the footprints inside the genkan didn't seem to have been made by shoes that had trodden in snow, so the conclusion was that they had been made before 9 p.m.

Additionally, according to Akiko, who had walked around the engawa at around 7 p.m. to close all the rain shutters, there hadn't been any footprints inside the genkan at that time. It was decided that the killer must have crept in between 7 and 9 p.m.—most likely while the wedding ceremony was underway in the main house. So far, this all seemed to make sense.

But what did the murderer do after sneaking into the house? Again, please take a look at the sketch. There's a little storage closet just opposite the toilet. It is believed that the murderer hid in there. This particular closet was filled with discarded bedding and some cotton filling that had been removed from old futons. There were clear imprints left in the cotton wadding that indicated somebody had been lying there. Not only that, but the scabbard of a katana, presumably the one that had been used as the murder weapon, was lying on the closet floor.

This sword belonged to the Ichiyanagi family and had been on display on a shelf in the tokonoma of the larger room earlier that day. The killer must have taken it into the closet with him. This means that during the sake ceremony the katana was already missing, but nobody noticed, probably because the folding screen had been placed in front of the alcove.

It seems strange though that the killer waited until 4 a.m. to commit the murder. After all, the bride and groom had gone to bed around 2 a.m. There were many theories about this, but the most persuasive argued that since it was their wedding night, Kenzo and Katsuko were probably not in a hurry to go to sleep, and the killer wanted to wait for them to drop off before attacking. Well, this was the most accepted theory, but I'd like you to take one more look at the location of that closet.

Between that closet and the larger tatami room where the newly-weds were sleeping, there is only a single wall. The murderer must have been able to hear everything, feel everything that passed between them—every whisper, every breath, every sigh… This was the most nauseating aspect of this case. When Ginzo heard it from the police detectives, his face turned dark with anger and disgust.

Having waited until the couple fell asleep, the killer ventured out of the closet, blade drawn. He would have opened the shoji sliding doors that separated the west-side corridor from the tatami rooms and entered the bedroom area. But before that, he did something a little strange. Or so it seems.

The shoji door closest to the tokonoma alcove had been left open just a crack. After Katsuko finished her koto performance, Akiko of the branch family reported having placed the box containing the koto picks in the back right-hand corner of the tokonoma. But when the crime scene was discovered, the box of picks was found in the front left corner, right by the small opening in the shoji. The killer had evidently slid the door open a little, reached in through the opening and picked up the box. Then he had removed three koto picks from it, slipped them onto his fingers and put the box back in a different location.

The police came to this conclusion after examining the bloody three-fingered handprint on the gold-leaf byobu screen. I mentioned at the end of the previous chapter that there was something bizarre about this handprint, and now I can reveal that there were no prints at all left by the fingers, just scratch marks left by koto picks.

Perhaps this would be the right moment to remind you of the nature of koto picks. Unlike other kinds of musical picks or plectrums, the koto pick resembles a false fingernail attached to a ring. The ring slips over the finger, with the nail part covering the pad of the finger. In other words, if you were wearing koto picks, your fingerprints would be obscured. Knowing this, the killer had slipped koto picks onto his fingers before committing the murders... or so the police believed. As the three missing koto picks were found covered in blood on the shelf above the handbasin in the lavatory area, it seems to have been a reasonable conclusion.

So the killer with three koto picks on his hand and brandishing a katana, crept into the room where the newly-weds were sleeping. First he attacked Katsuko, who was sleeping on the side nearer the entrance, slashing her several times. There was evidence that Katsuko had struggled briefly, but with no great force; it seemed the blade of the sword had killed her almost immediately.

No doubt woken by the noise, Kenzo had sat up, only to be cut down by the killer with a blow that sliced open his arm. Undaunted, he had then thrown himself on top of Katsuko's body to protect her, at which point the killer ran him through with the katana, leaving the bridegroom's body, pierced straight through the heart, lying lifeless on top of his bride.

This was the scenario that Inspector Isokawa constructed in his mind, but there was a lot more that he didn't understand.

I have already mentioned that the koto had been brought to the bedside and appeared to have been played with bloody fingers, but why on earth had the murderer paused his attack to play a musical instrument? And then there was the bridge from under the broken string. Why was that missing and where had it gone? The investigators had searched the whole annexe building but it was nowhere to be found.

However, even more mysterious was the disappearance of the killer himself. How had he escaped? Every single door or window of the building had been sturdily locked from inside. There was not a single opening through which anyone—man or woman—could have squeezed.

And yet someone had killed Kenzo and Katsuko and, after playing the koto, had apparently gone out through the shoji doors on the west side and onto the engawa. He'd left the three bloody koto picks above the handbasin and, just inside the amado rain shutter that Ryosuke and Genshichi had broken with the axe, he'd dropped a small hand towel, crumpled into a blood-smeared ball. But that wasn't all—on the inside of the smashed rain shutter itself was a bloody handprint with only three fingers. But this time, the fingers were not covered by koto picks—the prints were faint but visible.

This piece of evidence suggested that the killer had made his escape through the rain shutters, or at the very least had tried to open them. The question was: had the shutter really been bolted shut before Genshichi had broken it with the axe? Ryosuke was the one who had reached inside and unlocked it, and he didn't take too kindly to suggestions that he might have been mistaken.

"The rain shutter was definitely bolted shut. Genshichi smashed a hole in it with the axe, just big enough for me to put a hand inside, reach in and slide the bolt. It's absurd to even suggest that the murderer could have escaped that way. And even if he did, how come there were no footprints out there in the snow? Genshichi and I are absolutely sure of that. Ginzo-san will back us up too."

Ginzo nodded his agreement, but at the same time, he fixed Ryosuke's face with eyes that held more than a hint of suspicion.

But let's back up for a moment…

Before dawn had broken that morning, Ginzo was standing with Ryosuke, staring in horror at the bodies of his niece and her husband. When the police began to arrive, Ginzo was finally able to tear himself away. It was around 7 a.m. and the weather had cleared up. The snow piled high on the roof of the main building was dazzling in the morning sun. The dripping of meltwater from the eaves of the house was becoming faster and faster.

But Ginzo was blind to the sight and deaf to the sound. His face was twisted in sorrow. And concealed deep beneath that sorrow was a deep sense of regret and anger.

Wordlessly, he started back towards the main house, but was interrupted by the arrival of Saburo. He'd stayed the night at Great-Uncle Ihei's house in K—, but now having got word from a servant about what had happened, he had hurried home. He looked pale, but it was his companion who caught Ginzo's attention—an elegant moustachioed gentleman in his mid-thirties. When the mistress of the house caught sight of him, she looked astonished:

"Oh, Ryuji! What are you doing here?"

"Mother, Genshichi just told me the dreadful news."

Of course he seemed upset, but at the same time calmer than expected under the circumstances.

"It's horrible! Dreadful! I don't know what to do. But, Ryuji, how are you here so quickly? When did you get back?"

"I just arrived from Fukuoka. The conference I was attending finished earlier than expected... I thought I would come to offer Kenzo my congratulations. I got off at N— station and had just stopped by Great-Uncle Ihei's house in K— to ask how the wedding had gone when Genshichi arrived..."

Ginzo had been watching the young man with great distrust, but as he heard these words, his eyes grew wider until his gaze was practically burning a hole in the side of Ryuji's face. The stare was so intense that Ryuji himself could hardly fail to notice it. He began to look uncomfortable.

"Mother, this man..."

"Oh, this is Katsuko's uncle. Ginzo-san, this is my second son, Ryuji."

Ginzo inclined his head and, without uttering a single word, returned to his room in the main house. For a while he just stood there thinking, but eventually he uttered a single sentence:

"That man's lying."

With that, he opened his suitcase and took out a blank telegram. After a few moments, he began to write.

KATSUKO DEAD. SEND KINDAICHI.

He addressed it to his own wife, then set out for the K— town post office.

CHAPTER 6

A Sickle and a Koto Bridge

"This is a hell of a case. Downright creepy, if you ask me. I've been doing this job a long time, and no matter how grisly or blood-spattered, there's not much that can surprise me any more. But the more I think about this one, the more unsettled I feel. Hey, Kimura, what do you make of the killer leaving footprints on the way in, but not on the way out?"

Detective Inspector Isokawa had pulled a desk out onto the engawa of the annexe house and was painstakingly trying to piece together some torn-up scraps of writing paper. His detective sergeant, Kimura, was assisting.

"Inspector, how about we look at this whole case more simply?"

"How do you mean, *simply*?"

"What if this Ryosuke character is lying? If we decide that, then there's nothing mysterious about it at all. Whether the screen was bolted shut or not—he's the only one who knows the truth. He's free to lie about it as much as he likes."

"Well, I suppose you've got a point, but then we've got the footprint problem."

"Inspector, shouldn't we concentrate on one thing at a time? We can check the garden again later for footprints. But let's focus on this for now—if Ryosuke is lying to us, then the question is: why?"

"Do you have any thoughts on the matter?"

"I think that he knows more than he's saying. I suspect he knows who the killer is."

"Still, whether he knows who the killer is and whether the shutters were locked or not are two separate questions."

"I don't think so. Or rather that's making it too complicated. You know, I just don't like that man. There's something sneaky about him."

"You can't go around judging people on first impressions. That's how mistakes get made."

That said, Inspector Isokawa's own impression of Ryosuke was far from positive.

All of the siblings from the head Ichiyanagi family had the appropriate appearance and bearing to be called descendants of the honjin. Even the good-for-nothing Saburo, with his indifferent attitude, was in his own, albeit lazy way, clearly the son of a well-to-do family. Ryosuke did not compare favourably at all. He was short and skinny, and looked older than his years. He had a fussy, finicky manner, and there was something a little coarse about him. You could see all of this if you looked in his eyes; those eyes that were constantly moving, forever checking out other people's expressions. At first glance you'd take him for timid, but in fact he was cunning—someone who never seemed to let down his guard.

"He's head of the branch family, right?"

"Right. He'll never inherit anything. The one who was murdered, Kenzo, was a scholarly type, and didn't really bother himself with family business. This Ryosuke's got quite a reputation for managing the business and profiting from it."

"What about that Ryuji? It seems very fishy that he just happened to arrive home this morning."

"Ah yes, that one. Rumour has it he's quite a good type. The folk in the village reckon he's easy to get along with. It seems he's employed by an Osaka hospital, and had just returned from a conference at Kyushu University. It would be a very simple thing to check on, so I doubt very much he's lying."

"Um… By the way, what you said just now: that you think Ryosuke might be protecting the killer… you mean that Ryosuke knows this three-fingered man? According to the okamisan at Kawada's, he was nothing but a tramp. A seedy-looking type."

Kawada's was the name of the cheap tavern that was mentioned at the opening of this story—the place where the three-fingered man had first been seen.

At this point, Inspector Isokawa had just finished his initial questioning of the Ichiyanagi family members. And so it followed that he had already heard all about the mysterious three-fingered man. It was Saburo who told him; as soon as he heard that a three-fingered handprint had been left in the annexe house, he couldn't wait to tell the inspector the tale he had heard at the barber's shop.

For Isokawa's part, as soon as he heard Saburo's story, he dispatched a police officer to Kawada's. The officer returned with a full description of the man, and the glass that he had drunk from. The okamisan had been true to her word—repulsed by the man's appearance, she hadn't used the glass since. Thanks to these actions, the three fingerprints were still clearly visible on the surface of the glass. Inspector Isokawa sent it straight off to be analysed.

When Saburo's story was repeated to Ryosuke's wife, Akiko, she recalled the strange man who had turned up at the kitchen shortly before the wedding. The police questioned old Nao, the servant, and all the others who'd been in the kitchen at the time, and determined that it had been the same man. They also heard from Akiko how the message the man delivered had been torn up and the scraps stuffed into the sleeve of Kenzo's kimono.

The detectives had obtained the kimono that Kenzo had been wearing at the time of his death, examined the sleeves, and discovered the shredded note. And that was what Inspector Isokawa and Sergeant Kimura were now busily trying to reassemble.

"Kimura, we're almost there. Have you got the piece that goes here? No, that's not it… This one looks right. Now just two more… There and… there. That's it!"

Fortunately, not a single scrap of the shredded notepaper had gone missing, and the detectives had succeeded in piecing together the whole thing. However, the paper turned out to be covered in pencilled squiggles, which seemed to squirm before their eyes.

"What weird handwriting! Kimura, this first word?… What do you think that is?"

"I think it's the character for 'island', sir."

"Island?… Yes, now you say it, it does look like island. 'The island pact or agreement', isn't it? The island agreement… what's that next word?"

"I think it says 'short'. 'Will shortly' maybe?"

"Yes, yes. Will shortly be… is that 'executed'? Now, I can't read the next word either."

The handwriting was so poor to start with, added to which the paper had been torn into so many tiny pieces, that it took skill to read anything at all. However, the two men worked patiently together, and eventually came up with a message.

The island agreement will shortly be executed. We agreed to it—be it under cover of night, by surprise attack, by whatever means—an agreement was made.

From the one you call your "Mortal Enemy"

The two detectives were speechless for a few moments.

"Sir, this is a warning," said Kimura eventually. "It's advance notice of a murder."

"It looks that way. It's a clear threat. And several hours after taking delivery of this letter, he was murdered. Damn it! This case has turned even nastier."

Inspector Isokawa stood up, holding the glued-together message.

"Let's go and make some enquiries at the main house. This 'island agreement'—we'd better find out if Kenzo ever spent time on an island somewhere."

Just as the inspector was sliding his feet into a pair of geta sandals, someone called his name. It was the junior detective tasked with going over the outside of the west end of the building with a fine-toothed comb.

"Inspector Isokawa, could you please come and have a look at this? I found something odd."

"What? More discoveries?"

The young detective directed him to a spot just under the eaves of the lavatory extension on the north-west corner of the building. (If you wouldn't mind referring once again to the sketch on page 49.) Someone had swept up some fallen leaves into a pile on the ground. The police officer pushed some of the leaves aside with the end of a stick.

"Take a look at that."

The inspector's eyes widened.

"Isn't that from a koto?"

"That's right, sir. The missing koto bridge. Someone dropped it out here. It looks like the killer passed this way while making his escape. I thought at first that he might have thrown it from one of the lavatory windows, but as far as I can see, they all have a fine wire mesh over them. The holes in the mesh are too small to fit a koto bridge through. That treetrunk ranma above the amado rain shutters: also impossible. You could throw the koto bridge through the gap but the angle's wrong—the lavatory wall would have blocked its trajectory towards the leaf pile. But there was one stroke of luck—because it fell into this pile of leaves and got buried, it hardly got wet at all. There's a bloody fingerprint still visible."

Inspector Isokawa looked up at the lavatory windows and then the ranma over the shutters. The young detective was right.

"Right, take care of this. Get it off for analysis. Have you found anything else?"

"Yes, one more thing. Over here."

The junior detective directed them to the huge camphor tree.

"There's that too," he said, pointing up into its branches. "See, around the height of the third branch from the bottom? There's a sickle stuck up there. I tried to climb up to get it but it's really stuck fast into the trunk and I wasn't strong enough to pull it out. I examined the handle and there's the name of a gardening company branded on it."

"The gardener must have forgotten it."

"It does look as if the grounds have been recently tended to. But up in a tree like that? I'd understand if they'd left some shears or something, but not a sickle. It's weird."

"I see what you mean."

The inspector paused to think.

"Leave the sickle up there for now. And... what else was it?... Ah yes, don't forget to get that koto bridge back to the station. And just in case, search really carefully around here one more time."

Inspector Isokawa made his way over to the main house, where he found the whole Ichiyanagi family assembled in the sitting room. Ginzo was there too in the corner, smoking a pipe. He'd been encamped in that position ever since returning from the post office that morning, hardly exchanging a word with anybody. He sat there, silently puffing on his pipe and listening to the whispered conversation of the others. Forgetting any sense of restraint or decorum, he was openly scrutinizing the family's expressions and behaviour. For the family's part, the presence of Ginzo there in their sitting room was as oppressive as an overcast sky in rainy season. Ryosuke and Saburo seemed particularly on edge: whenever they happened to glance in his direction, they hurriedly averted their eyes if he returned their gaze.

Only Suzuko had seen that there was something gentle and kind about this old man, underneath his angry exterior. She was behaving affectionately towards him, and right now was lying on the floor with her head in his lap.

"Hey, Uncle Ginzo?" she asked, pulling on his finger. "I've got something weird to tell you."

Ginzo glanced at Suzuko's face, a little confused.

"Yesterday, in the middle of the night I heard a koto playing. First of all it sounded like *plink plunk thrum thrum*, like someone had koto picks on their fingers and was really pulling like crazy on all of the strings. Then the second time I heard it was kind of *ping ping*, like someone was plucking at one string. Uncle Ginzo, do you remember?"

"Yes, I remember."

"Well, the day before yesterday, in the evening, I heard the same sound."

Ginzo looked at Suzuko in surprise.

"Suzuko-san, are you telling the truth?"

"Of course I am. And the sound was coming from the annexe."

"So the sound you heard two nights ago was the same thrumming, like someone pulling like crazy on the strings?"

"No. Not like that. Well, they might have made that sound first, but I must have been sound asleep then. That night I only heard the *ping ping* sound."

"Do you know what time you heard it?"

"I don't know what time it was. I was so scared I hid under my bedcovers. Coz that night there wasn't anybody in the annexe. And the koto was still over here. Uncle Ginzo, is it true that when a cat dies it turns into a ghost?"

That was how all conversations with Suzuko ended up. Just when she seemed to be making sense, she'd suddenly leap into the realm of fantasy.

And yet, it really seemed that two nights ago she had heard the same koto sound… Ginzo felt that there was something very significant about that information. He was just about to ask Suzuko to tell him more when Inspector Isokawa came in, and that was the end of the conversation.

"I have something I'd like to ask all of you," the inspector said. "Did Kenzo-san ever spend any time on an island anywhere?"

The Ichiyanagis looked at each other.

"Hmm... Ryo-san, what do you think?" said Ryuji. "Kenzo hadn't really been out anywhere at all recently, had he?"

"No, it doesn't have to have been recent," the inspector said hastily. "It could have been a long time ago. Did he visit an island? Did he stay on one for a while?..."

"Ah, in that case he probably did. When he was young, my brother used to like travelling. He used to go on walking trips all over the place. But what does that have to do with his death?"

Ryuji looked puzzled.

"Well, we believe that the island connection is important to solving his murder. It would be helpful if we knew the name of a particular island. The one mentioned here."

Inspector Isokawa produced the reconstructed note.

"There's a very mysterious message written on this paper. I'll read it out. Please tell me if it means anything to you."

The inspector proceeded to read the message aloud. When he came to the final phrase, *From the one you call your "Mortal Enemy,"* there was a faint cry. It was Saburo. Under the detective inspector's piercing gaze, and the questioning looks from the rest of his family, the colour drained from his face and he looked as jittery as a criminal caught red-handed.

CHAPTER 7

A Strategy Meeting

Saburo's strange behaviour had caught the attention of everyone in the room.

"Saburo, do you know something about this letter?" asked Ryuji, obviously displeased.

Under the pressure of everyone's attention focused on him, Saburo got flustered.

"I-I—" he stuttered, wiping the sweat from his forehead.

Inspector Isokawa's glare grew harder.

"Saburo-san, if you know anything at all, then you need to speak up. This is extremely important."

The inspector's tone was stern, and it put Saburo in even more of a state, but eventually he managed to speak.

"That phrase at the end of the letter, I... I've heard it before. *Mortal Enemy.* I've seen those words before."

"Seen them? Where did you see them?"

"In Kenzo's album. There was a photo with that written underneath. I... No name—just 'My Mortal Enemy'... At the time I thought the words were strange, so I recalled them straight away."

Itoko and Ryosuke exchanged a furtive glance. Ryuji looked troubled. From his spot in the corner, Ginzo kept a careful watch on all three.

"Where is this album you're talking about?"

"It should be in his study. My brother was always very

particular about letting people touch his things. I just happened to catch sight of that photograph."

"Madam, may I have your permission to search the study?"

"Of course you may. Saburo-san, please show the inspector the way."

"I'll go too," said Ryuji, getting up from his seat. Ginzo also got to his feet and followed the others.

Kenzo's study was to the left of the main house's entrance hall, in other words in the south-east corner of the building. It was a spacious Western-style room—about 200 square feet, the equivalent of twelve tatami mats in size, but it had been partitioned into two by a thin dividing wall. The smaller of the two areas was for Saburo to use as his own study, and he had his own separate door at the north end of the room. This meant that Kenzo had a space the equivalent of around eight tatami or about 140 square feet to himself. The east and north walls were covered from floor to ceiling with bookcases crammed with foreign books. Under the window on the south side was a large desk. Right in the middle of the two areas was a metal charcoal-burning heater.

"Saburo-san, where's this album?"

"On this bookshelf… around here somewhere…"

The things Kenzo used regularly were conveniently arranged on a bookshelf to the left of the desk. There was a photograph album, a series of diaries and some newspaper clippings, all neatly lined up. Saburo reached out to take the album, but Inspector Isokawa swiftly put out a hand to stop him.

"Just a minute."

The inspector stood for a moment surveying the contents of the shelf.

It appeared that Kenzo had been scrupulous about keeping his diary. Beginning in 1917 up to 1936, or last year, he had twenty volumes arranged in chronological order. Moreover, they had all been made by the same Tokyo company, and their size, binding and paper quality were identical. They revealed a lot about what kind of person Kenzo had been.

The inspector brought his face up so close to these volumes that he was practically rubbing his forehead on the bookshelf. He stared at them for a while, then eventually turned to face the others, a frown on his face.

"Someone has tampered with these diaries recently. These three volumes here, 1924, '25 and '26 are not properly aligned with the others. Also, all the rest have a very light layer of dust on them, but these three don't. And then there's one even stranger thing."

Inspector Isokawa very carefully took the three volumes from the shelf. He showed each one to the other men. Ginzo squinted to see better, but was mystified by what he saw. All three volumes were missing pages, apparently cut or torn out. The 1925 diary was missing around half of its pages. The binding was practically hanging off.

"Take a look. These pages have been cut out recently. Could you tell me how old Kenzo was between 1924 and 1926?"

"Kenzo turned forty this year, so in 1924 he would have been twenty-seven," replied Ryuji, using his fingers to count.

"So these were his diaries from the ages of twenty-seven to twenty-nine. What was he doing in those days?"

"He graduated from university in Kyoto when he was twenty-five, and stayed on there for the next two years as a lecturer. Eventually he became worried enough about the respiratory problems he'd been having that he decided to quit his job, and for the next three years he spent his time doing very little besides trying to recuperate. If you look in his diaries, there's quite a lot written about that time."

"So you're saying these volumes cover the period around when he gave up teaching and was being treated for pulmonary disease? I need to ascertain who cut out these pages, and why. And what happened to those missing pages, how did this person dispose of them? Like I said before, this looks like a very recent job... Hey, is anything the matter?"

The inspector turned abruptly to look at Ginzo, who was coughing rather pointedly and tapping the charcoal heater with his pipe. The inspector got Ginzo's meaning immediately. He strode briskly over to the heater and tugged open the metal door in the front. He gave a snort of satisfaction. The interior was piled high with the remains of burnt paper, some leaves of which still retained their original form.

"When was this heater last cleaned out?"

"There was nothing like that in it last night," said Saburo, peering inside. "I was in here yesterday evening until around seven, reading a book. I added more charcoal to it a few times. I did it myself so I'm absolutely sure there were no papers in it then."

Ginzo was watching Saburo's face carefully, his own betraying no emotion. Feeling Ginzo's eyes on him, Saburo blushed crimson.

"That's fine. I'll look into it more thoroughly later," continued Inspector Isokawa. "Please make sure none of you touches these burnt remains. So, Saburo-san, this must be the album you were talking about."

There were five photo albums in all. They each had the years written on the spine in red ink. Inspector Isokawa pulled out the one marked "1923 to 1926", laid it on the desk and very carefully began to look through it. He'd barely reached the fifth or sixth page when Saburo piped up.

"Inspector, that's it. That's the photo."

He was pointing to a business-card-size photograph, quite faded, creased and worn. All the other photos around it appeared to be amateur shots, probably taken by Kenzo himself, but this one was obviously taken by a professional photographer. It was the kind of official headshot photo you would use on something like a university entrance exam application.

The photo was of a young man of around twenty-three or -four years of age with close-cropped hair and wearing a shirt with a stand-up collar fastened by a brass button.

Underneath this picture was written in bold lettering "My Mortal Enemy". The handwriting was clearly Kenzo's own. The red ink had faded to a dull brown.

"Do any of you know who the subject of this photo is?"

Ryuji and Saburo both shook their heads.

"Saburo-san, you didn't ask Kenzo anything about the photo?"

"If I'd asked him something like that, I can't even express how angry my brother would have been. I had to keep secret even the fact that I'd seen it."

"My mortal enemy. It's a very extreme turn of phrase. Do either of you have any memories of an incident that could have sparked this reaction?"

"My brother was a very private person," said Ryuji, frowning. "He never let anybody see into his heart. If there had been such an incident, he probably wouldn't have spoken about it to anyone. It would have been his personal secret."

71

"Anyway, I'm going to borrow this photograph for now," said the inspector. He tried to peel it away from the page, but it was too firmly stuck down. Fearing that he might damage the photo if he pulled too hard, he took a pair of scissors, cut through the thick mounting paper around it and placed it carefully between two pages of his notebook.

I believe there was a review meeting at the police station in S— town that evening.

I confess I don't know much about police meetings. I only got the gist of what happened from Doctor F—'s notes, so I have used some artistic licence to piece together how things must have gone.

"...And this is what we know about the burnt pages from the diary."

(Of course, that would have been Inspector Isokawa.)

"As I have already mentioned, yesterday evening, shortly before the wedding ceremony, Akiko from the Ichiyanagi branch family went to the annexe house in search of Kenzo. At that time, Kenzo asked Akiko to close the rain shutters all around the annexe house, and left shortly before she did. Not long after, Akiko returned to the main house, but Kenzo, who should have been there before her, was nowhere to be seen. By then it was getting close to the time of the wedding ceremony and the lady dowager, Itoko, was becoming impatient, so she sent Akiko to look for him. Akiko claims to have found him in his study, burning something in the charcoal heater."

"I see," the chief inspector interjected. "So in fact the person who tore out and burned pages from the diary was Kenzo himself."

"That's correct. I've heard it's fairly common for people to get rid of old diaries and letters before getting married, but in this case there must be some significance in his doing it right before the ceremony was due to take place. In other words, the message written on that scrap of paper that Akiko took to him in the annexe house must have reminded him about something from his past. And he felt it necessary to destroy all records of it right away."

"So that's how you explain the burnt pages from his diaries?"

"Right. He appears to have taken great care to leave nothing of them behind. Every page is almost completely burnt. There are only these five—a very small percentage of the total—that have any legible bits left at all. Now I don't know whether this is even connected to our case or not, but I'm going to read this small selection for you. Unfortunately, the part with the date is all burnt off, so I can't be sure when it was written, but I think it was probably around 1925."

Inspector Isokawa had brought the five scraps of paper that were saved from the fire. Those words, which had so nearly been reduced to ash, held great significance. Doctor F— made a careful memo of what they contained. I'm going to copy his notes here for you.

1. *...on my way to the beach I went by the usual place. Ofuyu-san was playing the koto again. Lately I find the sound of that koto melancholy...*
2. *...that dog, that brute. I really despise him. I will despise that man for the rest of my life...*
3. *...Ofuyu-san's funeral. A desolate, mournful day. It's drizzling again here on the island. The funeral was...*

4. *...I'm thinking of challenging him to a duel. This inexpressible fury. When I think of the lonely death that she met, I could tear him limb from limb. I consider him my mortal enemy and I hate him, hate him, hate h...*
5. *...before I left the island, I paid one more visit to Ofuyusan's grave. I took some wild chrysanthemums and as I was praying, I thought I could hear the sound of a koto. Abruptly I...*

"I understand."

After reading over the legible writing on the diary pages himself, the chief inspector offered his personal analysis:

"It seems this Kenzo got close to some woman called Ofuyu on an island somewhere. This Ofuyu-san was deeply involved with another man who somehow caused her death. So that man became Kenzo's mortal enemy. And that man is our murderer."

"That's how it seems," said Inspector Isokawa. "There's probably a very long and complicated history behind the whole thing. It would help if we knew this man's name or even the name of the island, but of course the diary pages that could tell us that have been burned. We do know that in 1925 Kenzo was twenty-eight years old, and suffering from a mild bout of pneumonia. He was apparently travelling around the Seto Inland Sea, touring the islands in that region. I've asked the Ichiyanagi family which island this could have been, but nobody knows."

"But we do have that photo... Take it to the tavern where the three-fingered man first showed up."

"Naturally, it's already been done, sir. I showed it to the okamisan and the village official and the wagon driver who

74

was with them at the time, and all three swear it was the same man. Of course, they all say he was much older and thinner—wasted away—and that he had a large scar on his cheek, so that his appearance had changed a lot, but all three of them said they were certain it was the same man."

"So there's no doubt then. And after the man left the tavern that day no one saw him again?"

"Actually, someone did."

It was Detective Sergeant Kimura who spoke.

"He was spotted the same day by a peasant farmer by the name of Yosuke Taguchi, who lives near the Ichiyanagi place. He says he saw the man standing in front of the residence's main gate, peering in. Perhaps the man realized how suspicious he looked, because he asked in a really unconvincing way whether he was on the right road for H— village, and upon getting the answer, wandered off in that direction. Yosuke walked on, but when he looked back, the man was clambering up that steep hillside on the north side of the compound. It's reasonable to assume that he climbed up there to get a better view of the whole Ichiyanagi residence. This all happened ten minutes or so after he left the tavern."

"And that was the evening of the 23rd? Two days before the wedding?"

"That's correct."

"Incidentally, all the staff who were in the kitchen when the man turned up right before the wedding ceremony, and this what's-his-name, Yosuke Taguchi—have you showed the photo to all that lot too?"

"Naturally. But they weren't much use. They all said he had his hat pulled down and was wearing a mask over his nose and mouth. And the kitchen at the Ichiyanagi house is pretty dark…"

The chief inspector smoked a cigarette as he considered the case. Then he looked down at his desk where there was an assortment of articles lined up.

1. a glass
2. a katana sword
3. a scabbard for a katana sword
4. three koto picks
5. a koto bridge
6. a sickle

He looked over the items as he spoke.

"I assume this is the glass from that tavern. Fingerprints?…"

The young man in charge of forensic analysis responded.

"Should I give my report? I have a photo here. It shows that there were two sets of fingerprints on the glass. The first belongs to the okamisan; the second consists of only a thumb, index finger and middle finger, which leads us to believe they were made by the so-called three-fingered man. We found the same prints on this sword, the scabbard and the koto bridge. Additionally, the prints on the koto bridge were made in blood. The sword and the scabbard also had traces of Kenzo's fingerprints; the koto bridge had none besides the killer's. As for the koto picks, they should have had the killer's prints on their underside, but they were so completely soaked in blood that we weren't able to check for prints. And as you can see, the handle of the sickle is made of a very rough type of wood, so we were unable to find any clear prints on it either."

"Where did the sickle come from?"

"I'll explain," said Inspector Isokawa, getting to his feet.

"It was found embedded in a camphor tree in the garden of the annexe house. Upon investigation we found that a gardener had been working at the Ichiyanagi residence about a week before the murders. We asked him about the sickle and he told us he'd left it behind, but as for being stuck into the trunk of the camphor tree, he said it would be very unlikely that anyone would climb a tree with a sickle. I see no reason to doubt the gardener's word. So we are left with the problem of why it was stuck in the tree, and why the blade had been made so extremely sharp. We confiscated the sickle in the hope of finding how it could be significant in the case."

"Thank you. I see there are lot of unanswered questions. And what about fingerprints at the crime scene?"

"We discovered the killer's fingerprints at three locations. The first was inside the storage closet near the larger room, where we believe he had been hiding before the murder. Those had no blood on them. Then there were another two locations with bloody prints: the inside of the rain shutter and the supporting pillar on the south-west side of the larger room. These latter prints were in the most obvious location, but they were the last to be discovered. We missed them at first because the whole house had recently been painted red."

"So this confirms that there was definitely a third person, namely the killer, in the house? There's no chance that this was a lovers' suicide?"

"A suicide?" Inspector Isokawa looked dumbfounded.

"Ah, that's not my own opinion," the chief inspector added hastily. "I don't believe anyone could pierce their own heart with a sword and then throw the weapon out into the snow, locking the shutters again afterwards."

"But are you saying that somebody does support that preposterous theory? If you look at the crime scene, there's no possible way it could have been suicide. First of all, there's the position of the murder weapon in the ground. And then the koto bridge – it's clear that it was dropped there as the murderer escaped. Even if the rain shutters were open, it would be impossible to stand inside the house and throw either the katana or the koto bridge, for that matter, to land in the spots where they were found. Are you telling me that someone believes that could be done?"

"It was Seno. That man is always hoping cases turn out to be suicide so he doesn't have to pay up."

"Pay up?… Oh, that Seno! The insurance company agent. So how much was Kenzo covered for?"

"Fifty thousand yen."

"Fifty thousand?!"

The police inspector's reaction wasn't excessive. In those days, in a rural region like that, fifty thousand yen was a considerable sum.

"And when did he take out that policy?"

"Five years ago."

"Five years?… But why would a man with no wife or children need to take out such an expensive insurance policy?"

"It seems that Kenzo has a younger brother by the name of Ryuji. Five years ago, at the time of Ryuji's wedding, the estate was divided between the brothers. The third brother, Saburo, was incensed because his portion was too small. He kicked up such a fuss that Kenzo decided to make Saburo the beneficiary of his fifty-thousand-yen life insurance policy."

"So Saburo stands to receive fifty thousand yen."

Inspector Isokawa had a very strange sense of foreboding.

On the night of the wedding, Saburo had walked his great-uncle home to K— town, and spent the night there. In other words, of all the people concerned, Saburo had the clearest alibi, proof that he hadn't been near the scene of the crime. But perhaps that point would turn out to be of the greatest significance...

Inspector Isokawa sat there twisting his moustache.

CHAPTER 8

Kosuke Kindaichi

It was 27th November, or the day after the discovery of the Ichiyanagi family murder.

A young man alighted at N— station on the Hakubi Line, and came sauntering down the road towards K— town. He was around twenty-five or -six, of medium build, on the pale side, and he would have been completely unremarkable if it weren't for his unusual choice of clothes. He wore a matching set of short *haori* jacket and kimono in a kind of splash-pattern dye, with a traditional *hakama* skirt of narrow stripes over it. However, the haori and kimono were full of wrinkles, and the hakama, conversely, had lost any trace of its crisp pleats. His toenails were beginning to poke through the ends of his *tabi* socks, his wooden *geta* clogs were worn down, his hat had lost its shape… In short, for a young man in the prime of life he seemed shockingly indifferent to his appearance.

This youth crossed the T— river and approached K—. His left hand was stuck in his pocket, and in his right, he carried a walking stick. His haori was bulging at the chest; it appeared to be stuffed full of journals or notebooks.

In those days, Tokyo was full of characters like this one. You'd find them hanging around the boarding houses in the Waseda University area, or in the writers' room in theatres in the seedy part of town. This was the man that Ginzo Kubo had summoned by telegram: Kosuke Kindaichi.

In the collective memory of the villagers, even those most closely involved in the case, this young man is still something of an enigma.

"How could that scruffy-looking youth manage to do what a police inspector couldn't? I suppose they make them different up in Tokyo. Anyway, that was the gossip at the time."

This is how I first heard that the young man had played such an important role in the solving of the Honjin Murder Case. Since then I have pieced together all the different accounts, and have begun to believe that the youth with his apparently relaxed, easy-going demeanour had something of the Antony Gillingham about him. Please, Ladies and Gentlemen, don't be confused by my sudden throwing out of a foreign-sounding name—this is the lead character in the detective novel *The Red House Mystery* by my favourite British author, A.A. Milne. Antony Gillingham was also an amateur detective.

Milne first introduces the character of Antony Gillingham with these words:

He is an important person to this story, so that it is as well we should know something about him before letting him loose in it.

I will also adopt Mr Milne's approach and straight away offer you some insight into the character of Kosuke Kindaichi.

The family name Kindaichi is rather unusual; the reader will doubtless immediately think of the famous scholar of Ainu studies of the same name. I believe that particular Kindaichi was from the north-eastern Tohoku region of Japan, or perhaps Hokkaido in the far north. Kosuke Kindaichi hailed from somewhere in the same general area. He spoke that northern dialect with a strong regional accent, and additionally had a tendency to stammer.

At the age of nineteen he graduated from his local school, and with lofty ambitions made his way to Tokyo. He entered a certain private university, hung about in his digs in Kanda for a while, then before a year was up, decided that Japanese universities were boring and hopped on a boat to America. He had no particular purpose in mind, and when it transpired that there wasn't much to interest him in America either, he ended up wandering from place to place, supporting himself by washing dishes and the like. On a whim he tried some narcotic drugs and gradually got hooked.

If things had continued as they were going, he would have ended up one of those lost, drug-addicted Japanese immigrants, but something unusual happened. There was a famous and quite bizarre murder in San Francisco's Japanese community that had remained unsolved for a long time. And when a certain young drug addict by the name of Kosuke Kindaichi stumbled upon the case, he succeeded in solving it once and for all. Surprisingly, there was no bluff or deception involved in his methods. From the start he employed reasoning and logic in a focused attack on the case, leaving the local Japanese community astonished, nay, dumbfounded. Overnight the hitherto good-for-nothing drug addict became a hero.

It just so happened that at the time all this occurred, Ginzo Kubo was visiting San Francisco. He'd had initial success with his fruit farm in Okayama Prefecture, and was planning a further venture. Ladies and Gentlemen, I'm sure you have memories from before the Second World War of enjoying a bag of Sunkist-brand raisins. Well, many of the grapes used by this brand were cultivated by Japanese farmers in California. Ginzo had got it into his head to try to grow the same grapes in Japan, and had come to San Francisco to observe the farming techniques. One evening he attended a meeting of Japanese residents and was introduced to Kosuke Kindaichi.

"Don't you think it's about time to stop messing with those drugs? Shouldn't you apply yourself to some kind of study?"

"I've been thinking that exact thing. It turns out drugs aren't all they're cracked up to be."

"If you really mean it, I'd be prepared to pay your tuition."

"I'd appreciate that very much."

As he bowed his head to Ginzo, Kosuke gave it a good scratch, causing his already shaggy mop of hair to become even wilder.

Shortly after that, Ginzo returned to Japan, but Kosuke remained in America for three more years and finished college. When he finally returned to Japan, he alighted in Kobe and immediately headed to Okayama to see his benefactor, the man whom he now affectionately called "Uncle".

"Well…" Ginzo asked him. "What do you plan to do next?"

"I've decided to become a detective."

"A detective?…"

Ginzo stared for a moment in shock, but then recalling the incident from three years earlier, he thought, *Why not?*… This youth was never going to be the type to pursue a respectable career:

"I'm not really familiar with the business of being a detective," he admitted, "but I suppose like in the movies, they go around with a magnifying glass and a tape measure."

"No, I'm not going to use anything like that."

"So what tools are you going to use?"

"I'll use this."

Grinning, Kosuke tapped his head, his hair unkempt as ever. Ginzo nodded appreciatively.

"But no matter how much you plan to rely on your brains, you still need some capital to get started."

"I s'pose so. I guess I'll need about three thousand yen for office equipment and stuff. And more for the time being to live off. I don't imagine that the minute I put a sign up I'm going to be overrun with customers."

Ginzo wrote a cheque for five thousand yen and handed it to him. Kosuke took it, nodded his thanks and without another word, left for Tokyo. It wasn't long before he set himself up in that rather eccentric line of work.

As expected, Kosuke Kindaichi's detective agency didn't flourish right away. The correspondence that he sent Ginzo from time to time described his office as being like a ghost town, its sole resident barely able to stifle his yawns. To pass the time he apparently read mystery novels. It was often hard to tell whether these reports were serious or joking.

But about six months after he'd set up his detective agency, the tone of the letters to Ginzo began to change. And then one morning, out of the blue, there was a large photograph of Kosuke in the morning newspaper. Wondering what trouble his young protégé had got into this time, Ginzo read the article only to discover that Kosuke Kindaichi, private detective, had managed to solve a major case, a crime that had been famous throughout Japan, and was being honoured in the paper for his distinguished service to the nation. They had printed a quote from the great detective himself.

"The police investigate footprints and look for fingerprints. I take the results of these investigations and by piecing together all the available information logically, I am able to reach a conclusion. Those are my methods of deduction."

Ginzo recalled how Kosuke had told him he'd use his head rather than tape measures and magnifying glasses, and smiled with satisfaction.

How was it that Kosuke had been visiting Ginzo's house at the time of the Ichiyanagi murder case? Well, there had been another major crime, this time in the city of Osaka, and Kosuke had been called from Tokyo to investigate it. He'd managed to solve the case unexpectedly fast, and, as he hadn't visited for a while, decided to continue on to Okayama Prefecture and take a short break at Ginzo's house. After seeing Ginzo and Katsuko off to the wedding, he had decided to take it easy for a few days until Ginzo returned. When he got Ginzo's telegram he'd set off immediately.

The distance from the part of Okayama where Ginzo had his orchards to the Ichiyanagi home in O— village was only about twenty miles, but the public transportation system was rather inconvenient. Kosuke had to take the Tamashima road to the Sanyo railway line and then at Kurashiki change to the Hakubi Line, arriving finally at N— station. After that, he had to walk another two and a half miles back in the direction he'd come from. It was the same route that Ginzo and Katsuko had taken on the wedding day.

Kosuke had just crossed the T— river and was approaching the main highway at K— town when he heard shouting. Several people were yelling and cursing. There was a curve in the road ahead and he ran on to see what the fuss was about.

When he rounded the bend, he saw that right at the end of the main K— shopping street, a public bus had run into a telegraph pole. A large crowd had gathered. Kosuke drew near just as the injured passengers were being carried out of the vehicle. From the conversations he could hear, Kosuke learned that the driver had swerved to avoid an ox cart and had collided instead with the pole.

Kosuke had seen the same bus back at N— station, and about half of its passengers had arrived on the same train as he had. If he had taken that bus, he would have met with the same misfortune. He was just moving on, counting his blessings, when his eye was caught by the figure of a woman who was being carried out of the wreck. He'd seen her before.

As I explained just now, early that morning Kosuke had travelled from Tamashima and then east on the Sanyo Line before changing to the Hakubi Line at Kurashiki. This woman had also changed trains at Kurashiki, although she had arrived from the opposite direction. She'd been sitting in the seat across from Kosuke and had seemed anxious and jittery.

The woman appeared to have bought several local newspapers along the way, and they were piled in her lap. She was reading intently and when Kosuke saw that she was absorbed in the reports of the Ichiyanagi family killings, he had taken another good look at her face. He guessed she was around twenty-seven or -eight. She was dressed in a rather plain kimono and a purple hakama. Her hair, although tied up in a traditional chignon style, was terribly frizzy, and she had a noticeable squint; she was far from what he would have called a beauty but she had the air of someone intellectual, which made up for her plainness. Kosuke would have guessed her to be a teacher at a girls' school.

Kosuke suddenly remembered that the bride, Katsuko, had also been a girls' schoolteacher. Perhaps this woman might be connected to Katsuko in some way? If he spoke to her he might be able to get some information that would help him with the case, but there was something stand-offish about her demeanour. Before he managed to strike up a conversation, they had arrived at N— station and he'd missed his chance.

It was definitely this woman who was being lifted now from the crashed vehicle. What's more, she appeared to have suffered the worst injuries of anyone. She was so completely pale and limp that Kosuke wondered for a moment if he should accompany her, but just then he happened to overhear a conversation in the crowd, and it stopped him dead in his tracks.

"Have you heard? They say the three-fingered man turned up again at the Ichiyanagi place last night."

"So they say. The police have been in a right flap about it since early this morning. Be careful—they've cordoned off the whole area. If they catch you hanging around looking shifty, they'll pick you up right away."

"What are you talking about? I've got all five of my fingers. But now that you mention it, where d'you think he could be hiding?"

"He's probably camped out in those hills somewhere between here and H— village. They say they've got together a group of young men from over there to go hunting him in the hills. Anyhow, sounds pretty serious."

"It's like there's some sort of divine punishment being wreaked on that family. The way Sakue-san met his death— and didn't Ryosuke-san's father, the old head of the branch family, commit *seppuku* in Hiroshima?"

"Right. There was an article about that in today's paper. Saying 'the blood of the whole clan is cursed' or something... You know it's always felt like that family has had some kind of shadow hanging over it."

As a matter of fact, the curse that the K— residents were talking about had indeed been mentioned in that morning's paper and so Kosuke already knew all about it. This is how the story went...

Sakue, the father of Kenzo and the other Ichiyanagi siblings, had passed away around fifteen or sixteen years earlier, or shortly after Suzuko was born. But it hadn't been a normal kind of death. Sakue had been known for his gentleness and understanding, but he also used to fly into blind rages. He'd reportedly got into a dispute over farmland with someone in the village. This quarrel festered over time until finally one night, Sakue attacked his adversary with a sword and killed him. Sakue also suffered a severe injury in the fight and died at home that same night.

The village elders had begun connecting that past incident with the current murder case, and had even embellished the story, claiming that the cursed Muramasa katana that Sakue had used to kill his opponent that night was the very same sword that had been used to murder Kenzo and Katsuko. They were shamelessly claiming that the Muramasa had somehow cursed the whole Ichiyanagi family, but in fact there was no truth in the tale at all. The katana that Sakue had used back then wasn't the same one at all. Moreover, that sword had been offered to Bodaiji Temple after the incident. According to police records, the katana that had been used by the murderer of Kenzo and Katsuko was a Sadamura. However, it was understandable that the newspaper editors would get excited and use phrases such as "cursed blood", since, famously, Sakue's younger brother Hayato, the head of the branch family and father of Ryosuke, had also died violently and by the sword.

Hayato Ichiyanagi was a military man. During the Russo-Japanese war of 1904–5, he had been a captain stationed in Hiroshima. However, he bore the responsibility for an internal scandal and ended up taking his own life by seppuku—ritual disembowelling with a sword. At the time it was considered admirable that he felt such a strong sense of responsibility, but all the same seppuku was an overreaction, people said. For something so relatively trivial to have been the trigger for suicide meant that he was hypersensitive to the point of being neurotic. The real cause of his suicide was considered to be this character flaw. To sum up, the Ichiyanagi family had suffered for generations from stubborn, headstrong men and their intense personalities.

Setting that aside for now, this was the first Kosuke Kindaichi had heard of the three-fingered man making another appearance at the Ichiyanagi residence. He knew he shouldn't hang around in K— town any longer—he needed to find out what had happened. He decided to leave behind the injured woman, but not without first confirming that she had been taken to the local Kiuchi Hospital. Then he made his way as quickly as possible to the Ichiyanagi home.

CHAPTER 9

The Cat's Grave

It was just before noon when Kosuke Kindaichi arrived at the Ichiyanagi residence in Yamanoya. There was a buzz of activity around the house, and policemen were everywhere. There was no doubting that there had been some kind of incident.

When Kosuke arrived, the Ichiyanagi family was assembled in the sitting room as usual, Ginzo in his customary corner. When he heard Kosuke's name announced, the older man was instantly filled with energy. He rushed to the front door to welcome his friend.

"It's so good to see you."

Ginzo's face betrayed an almost inappropriate level of happiness, given the circumstances.

"Uncle, I am so sorry—"

"Never mind all that for now. Come on, I'll introduce you to everyone."

The previous evening, Ginzo had announced that Kosuke Kindaichi would be arriving the next day, so that the assembled family members were all curious to meet this famed character.

Unfortunately, the man who showed up was a far from impressive figure: a scruffy youth barely older than Saburo, with bird's-nest hair. Everyone was a little taken aback, but Suzuko couldn't help herself.

"What, *you*'re the famous detective?" she asked.

Stunned into silence, the dowager Itoko, Saburo and Ryosuke all stared at the figure before them. Only Ryuji thanked him politely for making the long journey.

Introductions over, Ginzo took Kosuke to his room and did his best to explain everything that had happened since the night before last. Kosuke already knew some of the details from the newspaper, but there was much that he was hearing for the first time. When he'd finished, Ginzo had this to add:

"…And at this moment, they believe that this mysterious three-fingered man is the killer, but there's a lot more that I don't understand. First of all, Ryuji—he turned up unexpectedly early on the morning after the murders, walking into the grounds with Saburo, saying he'd just got back from Kyushu. But I could swear that when I travelled from Tamashima with Katsuko one day earlier, he was on the same train."

Kosuke let out a low whistle.

"So he's hiding the fact he was in the neighbourhood at the time of the murders."

"That's right. He doesn't know that I saw him on the train, but I am sure that from the night of the 25th to the morning of the 26th he was right here. What I don't know is why he's lying about it. For starters, if he was here in the neighbourhood on the evening of the 25th, why didn't he attend his brother's wedding? I can't fathom it."

Ginzo glared angrily in the direction of the sitting room.

"But it's not only that Ryuji!" he spat out. "Everyone in this house is weird. I can't help feeling they're deliberately hiding something. I think they're protecting each other. Or they all suspect each other. There's a suspicious smell in the air and it's getting right up my nose."

Kosuke listened attentively to every word, noting that his friend's tone was unusually vitriolic.

"By the way, Uncle," he said, as if it had only just occurred to him, "on my way here, I overheard people saying that the three-fingered man had appeared again last night. Is that true? Did something else strange happen?"

"Yes. And it was really bizarre. Suzuko is the one who saw him."

"What happened?"

"Well, it's Suzuko's story, and she's not all that reliable… My theory—it doesn't explain everything, but I believe she might be a sleepwalker."

"A sleepwalker?…"

Kosuke's interest was piqued.

"Yes. There's no reason for her to have got up in the middle of the night and gone to visit her cat's grave."

"Cat's grave?…"

Kosuke was even more fascinated. He laughed in delight.

"Uncle, this is some tale. Sleepwalkers and cat graves. It's quickly turning into a ghost story. Tell me more."

"No, no. I'm sorry, I'm not explaining myself properly. Here's what actually happened…"

Ginzo explained to Kosuke how the previous night—or rather in the early hours of the morning—they had all been awakened by yet another terrifying scream on the Ichiyanagi property. After the events of the previous night, Ginzo was swift to leap out of bed and open his room shutters. From the direction of the annexe house, a figure came stumbling towards him.

Ginzo ran straight out into the garden barefoot just in time to catch Suzuko, who collapsed into his arms. She was wearing a flannel nightgown, and was pale and trembling. She too was barefoot.

"Suzuko-chan, what is it? What are you doing out here like this?"

"Uncle, I saw it. I saw it. A ghost. I saw a three-fingered ghost."

"A three-fingered ghost?"

"Yes, I did. I saw it. Uncle, I'm frightened. I'm frightened. It's over there. Over by Tama's grave."

That was when Ryuji and Ryosuke came running. Saburo turned up a moment later.

"Suzuko, what are you doing wandering around out here at this time?" asked Ryuji sharply.

"But, but... I... I went to visit Tama's grave. And then... then suddenly a three-fingered ghost came—"

At that moment, the dowager Itoko appeared from the same direction that Suzuko had come, looking worried and calling Suzuko's name. Suzuko burst into tears and ran to her. The four men looked at each other, then Ginzo spoke.

"Shall we go and take a look?"

Without waiting for a reply, he walked off.

"I'll... I'll go get a lantern."

Saburo ran off but soon caught the others up, a lantern in his hand.

In the far north-eastern corner of the grounds, stretching from the fence that separated the annexe house from the main house to the boundary of the property, there was a thick grove of tall Japanese elm and oak trees. Scattered all around were piles of fallen leaves. In the midst of these leaves was the gently rounded mound of a home-made grave; on the marker written in childish handwriting, "Tama's Grave".

Stuck in the ground by this marker were three or four white chrysanthemums.

The four men searched the grove of trees, but there was no mysterious figure. They also used the light of Saburo's lantern to examine the ground closely, but the layer of fallen leaves was so thick it was impossible to make out anything that resembled a footprint. Finally, they split up and searched everywhere throughout the grounds, but there was no intruder anywhere.

"At that point, we all went back to the sitting room and started questioning Suzuko. We tried to get her to answer specific questions but the poor girl wouldn't stop babbling. She claimed she was out there paying her respects at the cat's grave, but it's just too bizarre to be visiting a grave in the middle of the night. That's what leads me to believe that the girl might be a sleepwalker. I think she may have been traumatized by the unpleasant and unexpected death of her pet kitten, and that led her to wander outside in her sleep to visit the grave. When she came across a suspicious-looking man out there, the shock caused her to wake up. I think she was in a state somewhere between dream and reality when she says she saw a strange-looking man crouching by the cat's grave. This man had most of his face completely concealed by a mask but it looked to her as if there was a gash by his mouth. Suzuko screamed and tried to run away. The man stuck out his right hand as if he were trying to grab her, and there were only three fingers on it… At least that's what Suzuko claims. I may have told you before that the girl is a bit strange in the head. She's rather slow for her age. You could say that her whole story is unreliable, but out of everybody in this family, Suzuko is the one I trust the most.

At the very least, she never tells a deliberate lie. So if she says she saw a man then she really saw him. And on top of that there is evidence that the three-fingered man was around here last night."

"Evidence? May I ask what evidence?"

"After dawn, we went back to the cat's grave to take another look around. We were hoping perhaps to find some footprints this time. Unfortunately, again because of the fallen leaves, we didn't find any. However, we did find something else even more useful. Fingerprints. Three fingerprints, to be exact."

"So where were these fingerprints left?"

"On the grave marker. There were three muddy finger-prints, clear as day."

Kosuke pursed his lips and let out another low whistle.

"And those fingerprints were definitely those of the three-fingered man?"

"Right. A police officer came first thing this morning and confirmed they matched all the prints found before. So there's absolutely no doubt whatsoever that last night the three-fingered monster was roaming the Ichiyanagi estate again."

Ginzo looked at Kosuke defiantly, but somewhere beneath the surface he clearly had misgivings.

"This cat's grave-marker, how long has it been there?"

"Since yesterday evening, it seems. The cat's remains were originally buried there the day before yesterday on the morning of the 25th, the day of the wedding, but there wasn't time to make a marker of any kind. And so yesterday, Suzuko pestered Saburo to make one. It seems that yesterday evening Suzuko and the maid, Kiyo, went out and set up the marker. Kiyo swears that there were no muddy fingerprints on it at that time. And it is just made of plain, unfinished wood, so

95

muddy fingerprints were something they'd have noticed right away."

"So the three-fingered man was here again last night. But why did he come back? And more to the point, why on earth did he touch the marker on a cat's grave?"

"Saburo had a theory that the killer had left something behind by mistake, and that he came back to find it. To which Suzuko added that someone had been digging in the grave. She said that the shape of the burial mound was different from yesterday. So the police immediately dug the grave up again—"

"Did they find anything?"

"No, nothing in particular. Just the home-made coffin that held the cat's remains... Apart from that nothing out of the ordinary."

"And the body of the cat was buried the morning of the day before yesterday, right?"

"Correct. And the wedding was that evening. Suzuko's mother and brother scolded her in the afternoon saying leaving the corpse lying around was bad luck, and Suzuko told them she'd already buried it in the early morning of the 25th. As I've said, I believe everything the girl says."

It seems that shortly after this conversation Kosuke went to check out the area in question behind the annexe house.

It's hard to believe that in a high-profile murder case such as this one, someone from outside the police force would be permitted to wander about the crime scene in this way, but somehow Kosuke Kindaichi managed it. This was a point that the members of the Ichiyanagi family, not to mention the villagers, found extremely odd. One of the elders who told me this story explained it the following way:

"That young man would whisper something to a police officer, and the officer would immediately look impressed. They'd all fall over themselves to help him. He was such a famous character already by that point."

This was one of the ways in which the young man achieved an almost mystical status among the people of the village. But according to F—, it was because he carried a letter of introduction from a high-ranking official:

"Before Kosuke Kindaichi came to this village, he'd been to Osaka for some sort of investigation. It was a grandiose affair apparently and he'd been handed some sort of identification papers by an official of the Home Ministry Police Affairs Bureau. He brought those with him, and I reckon having official papers on you is more effective than carrying a talisman from a shrine. The chief inspector and all of the judiciary were thoroughly awestruck."

However, my personal speculation is that it was not only because of this letter of recommendation from the ministry that the police and the judiciary showed him such extraordinary goodwill. From all the different accounts I've heard, people were charmed by the young man's relaxed manner and unaffected stammer. In addition, he endeared himself by always pitching in and helping when necessary.

The officer in charge of this case, Inspector Isokawa, was one of the many who would fall under Kosuke Kindaichi's spell. That morning he had been giving orders to the young men in the village, but he returned to the Ichiyanagi residence just after midday and was introduced to Kosuke. He was immediately taken with the personality of this young man, so much so that he went ahead and discussed the case with him, revealing what he had discovered so far.

Out of all the elements of the case, those that interested Kosuke the most were the photograph of the three-fingered man from Kenzo's album and the partially burnt diary pages that had been found in the charcoal heater. As he listened to the inspector's account he was grinning from ear to ear with delight, burying his hand in his messy thatch of hair to scratch his head, as was his habit whenever he got excited.

"Th-that photo and the burnt pages, where are they now?"

"At S— town police station. If you'd like to take a look, I can have them sent over for you."

"Th-that would be wonderful. Are all the other photo albums and volumes of the diary still in the study?"

"They are. I'll show you, if you like."

"Y-yes. If you could."

The inspector showed Kosuke into Kenzo's study, upon which the young detective pulled Kenzo's albums and volumes of his diary out at random and riffled through the pages. However, he was careful to return each one to its original spot on the bookshelf.

"Think I'll look at these more carefully later," he said. "Could you take me to the scene of the crime now?"

The two men were on the way out of the study when Kosuke stopped abruptly right in the doorway.

"Inspector?"

The young man was rooted to the spot and there was a curious expression on his face.

"Inspector, wh-why didn't you tell me?"

"About what?"

"Look! Th-those books crammed into the bookcase over there... they're all mystery novels!"

"Mystery novels?… Well… yes. Yes, they are. But what do mystery novels have to do with the case?"

But Kosuke didn't reply. He made straight for the bookcase in question, and stood there breathing heavily, intently scanning the shelves of detective novels.

Kosuke's amazement was in fact understandable. The collection comprised every book of mystery or detective fiction ever published in Japan, both domestic and foreign. There was the whole collection of Arthur Conan Doyle, Maurice Leblanc's Lupin series, and every translated work that the publishers Hakubunkan and Heibonsha had ever released. Then there was the Japanese section: it began with nineteenth-century novels by Ruiko Kuroiwa, and also featured Edogawa Ranpo, Fuboku Kozakai, Saburo Koga, Udaru Oshita, Takataro Kigi, Juza Unno, Mushitaro Oguri all crammed in together. And then as well as Japanese translations of Western novels, there were the original, untranslated works of Ellery Queen, Dickson Carr, Freeman Wills Crofts and Agatha Christie, etc. etc. etc. It was a magnificent sight: an entire library of detective novels.

"W-who does th-this collection b-belong to?"

"It's Saburo's. He's an avid reader by all accounts."

"Saburo?… Saburo?… Ah, Saburo's the one you were telling me is going to get K-Kenzo's life insurance payout. And he's th-the one with the firmest alibi."

And with that, Kosuke began to scratch madly at his scalp, his hair becoming more tangled by the second.

CHAPTER 10

A Conversation about Detective Novels

After the murder case was solved, Kosuke Kindaichi would often talk about this moment:

"To tell the truth, at first I didn't have much interest in this case. When I read the newspaper articles, it appeared it all hung on capturing this suspicious three-fingered man. I came to help solve this crime out of duty to my benefactor, but I was hoping to be done with such a mundane case as soon as possible. When I first passed through those gates to the Ichiyanagi residence, to be honest that was what I was thinking. The moment the case really became interesting to me was when I first laid eyes on Saburo's bookshelves full of Western and Japanese mystery novels. The Honjin Murder Case was essentially what is known as a 'locked room murder'. Among the books on Saburo's shelves were detective stories that also revolved around locked room murders. Should I chalk that up to mere coincidence? Not at all. Up until now it seemed that this might have been a crime of opportunity, but wasn't this in fact a case where the murderer had put a lot of careful thought into his or her plan? And was the blueprint of that plan in one of these very novels? Just to consider that possibility made me happier than I can tell you. The killer had submitted the problem of a locked room murder and dared us to solve it. It was going to be a battle of wits. Perfect. Challenge accepted! If it was brains and logic and wit that were required, I was ready to do battle."

At the time though, Inspector Isokawa found Kosuke's excitement childish.

"What's up with you? They're just detective novels. Didn't you say you wanted to see the crime scene? If we linger too long it'll be dark by the time we get there."

"Yes, that's true."

Kosuke had pulled five or six books from the shelf and was flipping through the pages. Inspector Isokawa's words seemed to bring him back to reality, and he put the books down with great reluctance. The kindly Isokawa could barely stifle his laughter.

"You're quite a fan, then?" he asked.

"N-no, not exactly. They're useful for reference, that's all. I'm just having a quick look. Anyway, let's go and see the crime scene."

That day the detectives and the rest of the police force were occupied with the manhunt up in the hills, so there was no one guarding the crime scene. The inspector had to break the seal on the front door himself before showing Kosuke into the annexe house.

The rain shutters were all closed so the interior was dim; just a pale light filtered in through the tree-trunk transom at the far end beyond the west-side engawa. November was almost over, and at dusk the unheated building was both physically and psychologically chilling.

"I'll open the shutters," said Isokawa.

"No, please leave them closed for now."

The inspector turned on the light in the larger tatami room.

"Apart from the bodies, everything has been left just as it was. The byobu folding screen was lying in that exact position, and the koto was here like a bridge between the pillar of the tokonoma alcove and the open shoji, and on this side of the screen were the bride and groom fallen on top of each other."

The inspector proceeded to explain the exact position of the two bodies. Kosuke listened carefully, expressing the odd *Hmm* and *I see*.

"And so the bridegroom fell with his head down here around the bride's legs?" he asked.

"Right. Yes. He fell face upwards, her knees under his head. I can show you the photos later, if you like."

"Ah yes, please."

Kosuke examined the three bloody koto-pick traces on the folding screen. Their outline stood out sharply against the brilliant gold leaf, and like overripe strawberries had darkened to a deep brownish hue. From the top end of these marks ran a long scratch, faintly bloody. The murderer must have accidentally grazed the screen with the bloody tip of the katana.

Next, he took a look at the koto with its one broken string. The streak of blood across the remaining strings had also begun to turn a rusty brown.

"And you found the missing bridge buried in a pile of leaves outside?"

"That's right. That's how we deduced that the killer definitely escaped through the west-side garden."

Kosuke looked over the twelve intact koto bridges, and immediately spotted something.

"Inspector, c-c-come and look at th-this."

Hearing Kosuke's stammer become more pronounced, Inspector Isokawa hurried over.

"Wh-what happened?"

Kosuke began to laugh.

"Inspector, you have quite a mean streak, don't you? There's no need to mimic my stammer."

"I apologize. I didn't mean to, it must be contagious. So, what did you find?"

"See here? This bridge? The other eleven are all alike, engraved with a depiction of a bird on a wave, but this one here is flat and smooth without any carving or decoration at all. In other words, this bridge doesn't belong to the Lovebird koto."

"Really? I hadn't noticed."

"By the way, what did the one you found in the pile of leaves look like? Like all the rest of these?"

"Yes, yes. There was a bird and wave pattern on it. But what do you think is the significance of a bridge from a different koto being mixed in with the others?"

"Well, I suppose it may be significant, but then again it might not. It might simply be that one of the original bridges got lost and they replaced it with whatever they happened to have... And now where is this closet? Behind the tokonoma here, right?"

Kosuke took a quick tour with Isokawa of the storage closet and lavatory area. Then he carefully examined the bloody fingerprints on the pillar in the larger tatami room and on the inside of the rain shutter. These had turned murky against the bright ochre red of the wood.

"I see. You didn't discover these right away because of the red paint?"

"No, we didn't, and as for the prints on the rain shutter, they're on the one closest to the shutter box at the end. That's the same shutter Ryosuke-san and the servant broke and slid open, so it ended up inside the shutter box, out of sight for most of our investigation. It wasn't until we closed all the shutters again that we found the prints."

By the fingerprints was the gaping hole that the servant, Genshichi, had made with his axe.

"I see. The people who were first on the scene would have had to slide this particular shutter across in order to get into the building, and therefore it would have been inside the box from the start."

Kosuke undid the bolt and slid the shutter to the side. The evening light came flooding into the house, temporarily dazzling the two men and making them blink.

"Well, I think that's about it for the interior of the house. Could you show me around the outside? Ah, just a moment… Is this the transom that Genshichi looked in through?"

With nothing but his tabi socks on his feet, Kosuke ran out to the decorative stone basin in the garden and climbed up on it. He stood on the tips of his toes and peered in, but at that moment Isokawa came out carrying their shoes.

The two men set off around the garden area. Isokawa pointed out the spot at the base of the stone lantern where the katana had been stuck upright into the snow, and the pile of leaves in which the missing koto bridge had been buried.

"Thank you. And you say there weren't any footprints anywhere?"

"That's correct. Of course, by the time I got here people had been trampling all over this part of the garden. But Kubo-san swears that the snow was completely untouched when he discovered the murders."

"I see. There weren't any footprints to analyse, so the first detectives and policemen to arrive on the scene felt free to stomp around as they pleased. Ah, and this is the camphor tree that the sickle was stuck in…"

Kosuke was darting here and there, taking in the scene from every angle.

"Yes, yes. I can tell that a gardener has been here lately. It's all perfectly tended to."

The pine trees that stood by the fence at the west end of the compound were neatly pruned, their heavy lower branches supported here and there by crutches made of pieces of young bamboo—a horizontal piece laid on top of a vertical one, bound together and to the pine branches by rope. Isokawa couldn't help laughing at the sight of Kosuke leaping from one ornamental rock to another to peer at each of the crutches.

"What's up with you? Do you think the killer hid inside a piece of bamboo?"

Kosuke grinned and began to scratch his head.

"Right, right. The killer may well have slipped through this bamboo to escape. Someone has hollowed it out so that you can see right through."

"What did you say?"

"When a gardener makes a support like this, he doesn't normally bother to grate away the inside of the bamboo."

He indicated the lowest branch of a large pine tree.

"And look—this particular branch has two bamboo crutches supporting it. You can tell by the way the rope has been tied that one of these has been put up by a professional gardener. But this crutch here was definitely done by an amateur."

Surprised, Isokawa moved closer to examine the bamboo.

"You're right. This horizontal piece is completely hollow. But what's its significance?"

"Well, first, the bizarre placement of the sickle in the tree trunk, and now, the hollowed-out bamboo, I can't think it's all just a coincidence. But I'm not quite sure yet what it could mean… Oh! Good evening!"

Inspector Isokawa looked around to see who Kosuke was calling to. Ryuji and Saburo were standing at the garden gate, and right behind them was Ginzo.

"May we come through?"

"Of course, of course. Hey, Inspector, you don't mind, do you?"

Isokawa turned back to look at Kosuke, who immediately lowered his voice.

"I think it's best not to mention the hollow bamboo for now," he said quickly, before heading towards the garden gate to welcome the three men. Ryuji and Saburo looked around with curiosity as they came into the garden. Ginzo followed behind with a perplexed look on his face.

"Have none of you been here since that day?"

"No," said Ryuji. "I didn't want to get in the way of the police. Saburo, you haven't been here either, have you?"

Saburo shook his head.

"We heard the story of what happened from Ryosuke. How's it going? Have you found out anything new?"

"Well, it's rather a baffling case. Inspector, would it be all right to open the shutters?"

Kosuke went back into the house the way he'd come out— through the open rain shutter and the west-side engawa—and slid open three of the shutters on the south side.

"Let's sit down here. Uncle, why don't you join us?"

Ryuji and Ginzo sat down with Kosuke on the opened-up engawa veranda, but Saburo remained standing, stealthily peering into the house. Inspector Isokawa stood a short distance away, keeping an eye on the assembled group.

Kosuke smiled broadly.

"So how about it, Saburo-san? Do you have a theory?"

"Me?"

Flustered, Saburo turned away from the house, and looked at the young detective.

"Do I have a?... Why do you ask?"

"Well, you seem to be an avid fan of detective novels. I'm sure with all your knowledge of mysteries you'll be able to solve the puzzle of this murder."

Saburo blushed, but at the same time there was a hint of contempt in his eyes.

"There's a big difference between mystery novels and reality," he began. "In mystery novels, the criminal always turns out to be one of the characters in the story. There's a limited pool of suspects. But in real life it's never that simple."

"You make a good point. But in this particular case, isn't the three-fingered man the only suspect?"

"I-I have no idea."

At this point, Ryuji decided to cut in.

"Are you also a reader of detective fiction?" he asked Kosuke politely, his face betraying no emotion.

"Yes, I do like to read mysteries. They're very helpful in my line of work. Of course, real life and fiction are very different, but the way of thinking—the logical thought process—is useful practice for anything life throws at you. What's more, what we have here is a locked room mystery. Right now, I'm

107

having to enlist all my brain cells, trying to recall if there hasn't been a detective story similar to this case."

"What do you mean by a 'locked room mystery'?" Ryuji asked.

"It's what you call a murder that has happened in a room where all the doors and windows are locked from the inside. The killer had no possible escape route. Mystery writers call it 'an impossible crime'. It appeals to authors to devise a method where a seemingly impossible crime can be carried out. The majority of mystery writers have written at least one in their lifetime."

"I see. That sounds fascinating. And what kinds of solutions do they come up with? Tell us about a few of them."

"Yes, of course. But I think we'd better ask Saburo here. Saburo-san, of all the locked room mysteries you've read, which did you find the most interesting?"

Saburo gave him a disdainful half-smile, then with his eyes on his brother's face, he replied somewhat lamely:

"Well, I kind of like Leroux's *Mystery of the Yellow Room*."

"Yes, of course it's a real classic. I'd call it a masterpiece of the ages, wouldn't you?"

"What's this *Mystery of the Yellow Room* about?" asked Ryuji.

Kosuke was quick to jump in:

"Well, in a room that is bolted shut from the inside, a young woman is seriously injured. Hearing her cry out, the young woman's father and servant come running, smash down the door and rush into the room, only to find signs of a struggle, blood everywhere and the victim on the verge of death. However, the attacker is nowhere to be seen. That's the gist of it. The reason this novel is considered a masterpiece is that there is no kind of machine or mechanism involved in the solution. There are all kinds of locked room mystery novels, but most of them include the use of a mechanical trick, which often turns out to be rather a disappointment in the end."

"What sort of mechanical trick?"

"Well, you know, the murder has been committed behind a locked door, but the killer used some sort of device—like a piece of wire or string—to turn the latch or slide the bolt closed again as he leaves. I'm totally unimpressed by that kind of thing. What about you, Saburo-san?"

"Yes, I agree with you. There's nothing quite like the *Mystery of the Yellow Room*'s trick. But then again, there are some sort of mechanical tricks that I find impressive."

"Like what?"

"Take the writer John Dickson Carr for example. Almost all of his novels are either locked room murder mysteries or some variation on a locked room, and they include some pretty good tricks. *The Mad Hatter Mystery*, for example, features a marvellously original one. By the strict rules of locked room mysteries, it would be considered mechanical, but of course, this being John Dickson Carr, the master, he didn't just use some cheap wire or string gimmick. *The Plague Court Murders* and some of his other mysteries involved mechanical tricks too, but he took great pains to camouflage them all. I am very sympathetic to authors in this regard. Personally, I don't feel such contempt for the mechanical genre of trick."

Saburo had got carried away with his own theories, but now he suddenly seemed to remember where he was.

"Oh dear, while we've been chatting away it's gone dark. Apologies. Whenever I start talking about detective stories, I get completely carried away and lose track of time."

Saburo shivered, but in the semi-darkness he shot Kosuke a sly glance.

Later that night the Ichiyanagi residence would be filled once again with the sounds of a koto…

CHAPTER 11

Two Letters

"Ko-san, Ko-san!"

Kosuke Kindaichi was rudely awakened from sleep, to see that it was still long before daybreak. The light was on in the room that he was sharing with Ginzo, and Ginzo himself was leaning over him, a grim expression on his face. Startled, Kosuke sat up in his futon.

"Wh-what is it, Uncle?"

"I thought I heard that strange noise again. Someone wildly playing a koto... I think it might have been a nightmare..."

The two men stayed perfectly still, listening, but there was nothing unusual to be heard. In a silence deep enough to count their own heartbeats, there was just one regular, rhythmic sound—the waterwheel up at the rice mill.

"U-uncle?"

Kosuke suddenly spoke in an urgent whisper. His teeth had begun to chatter.

"Two nights ago—the night of the murders—did you hear that waterwheel then?"

"The waterwheel?"

Ginzo was surprised by the question. He stared at Kosuke.

"Now that you ask me, I think I did hear it... Yes, yes, I definitely heard it. It's such a common sound that I didn't pay it any attention. But— Ah!"

Simultaneously, both men leapt to their feet and grabbed their clothes.

The koto had started up again. *Ping ping ping* as if someone was plucking at the strings. Then came a loud *twang* that seemed to split the air.

"D-drat, drat, drat… dammit, dammit, dammit," yelled Kosuke, getting all tangled up in his shirt.

The night before, Kosuke had gone to bed very late. As promised, Inspector Isokawa had brought the photo from Kenzo's album for him to look at, and he had stayed up until well after midnight examining it, along with the burnt remains of the diary pages, and the rest of the albums and diaries from the study. After that, he'd spent a couple of hours going through the detective novels that he'd picked out of Saburo's collection. It had been after 2 a.m. by the time he'd gone to bed. He was slower than usual to react.

"Uncle, what time is it?"

"Exactly half past four. The same as last time."

Hastily dressing, they slid open the rain shutters to find a heavy fog hanging in the air. They could just make out two figures apparently jostling each other. They seemed to be near the garden gate that led to the annexe house. Two voices could be heard: one was deep, that of a man, and it sounded as if he was scolding a sobbing woman. Peering through the fog, they saw that it was Ryosuke and Suzuko.

"What's the matter?" asked Ginzo, running to their side. "Suzuko-san, what happened?"

"It seems Suzu-chan had another sleepwalking episode," said Ryosuke.

"No, that's a lie! It's a lie! I came to visit Tama's grave. I'm not sleepwalking. You're lying! You're a liar!"

Suzuko began to sob again.

"Ryosuke-san, did you hear the noise just now?" asked Ginzo.

"I heard it. And when I came running out, I found Suzu-chan wandering about again."

Ryuji and Itoko materialized out of the mist.

"Is that you, Ryo-san? And Suzuko too? And what about Saburo? Have you seen him anywhere?" asked Itoko.

"Sabu-chan? He's bound to be asleep still."

"No, his bedroom was empty. Saburo was the first person I went to wake when I heard that noise."

"What's happened to Kindaichi-san?"

Just as Ginzo was looking around in the fog for his protégé, there was a piercing yell from the direction of the annexe house. It was Kosuke.

"Somebody call a doctor! Saburo's…"

The rest of his words were lost in the fog, but the effect was to turn everyone to stone.

"Saburo's been murdered!" cried Itoko, burying her face in the sleeve of her nightgown.

"Mother, go and sit down," said Ryuji. "Hey, Aki-san, will you look after Mother and Suzuko? And call the doctor?"

Akiko had appeared right at that moment. As she accompanied the other two women back to the main house, Ryuji, Ryosuke and Ginzo rushed together through the garden gate towards the annexe. Just as before, all the amado shutters were tightly closed. Light was filtering out through the ranma transoms and reflecting off the white of the mist.

"Th-there. Over there. You can get in through the west-side engawa."

Conversely, Kosuke's voice seemed to come from just inside the entrance of the building, at the east end. The three men

113

made their way around to the other end and found the broken rain shutter open. They hurried in and found both the shoji and fusuma sliding doors that divided the two tatami rooms wide open. They crossed through both of the tatami-mat rooms, to see the figure of Kosuke crouched down in the genkan entrance area. They rushed towards him but came to a halt at the sight before them.

On the earthen floor of the genkan lay Saburo curled up in a ball. His back was completely drenched in blood and he was scratching feebly at the door with his right hand.

For a moment Ryuji looked as if he'd been nailed to the spot, but then he pushed up his sleeves and, brushing Kosuke out of the way, squatted down next to his brother. He looked up at his cousin.

"Ryosuke-san, could you go to the main house and fetch my bag? And make sure the village doctor gets here as fast as he can."

"Is Sabu-chan going to… er?…"

"I think he's going to be all right. It's a pretty deep wound but… Just take care not to alarm Mother any more than necessary."

Ryosuke set off for the main house.

"Is there anything we can do to help?" asked Kosuke.

"No, best to move him as little as possible. Ryosuke'll be right back with my doctor's bag."

There was something brusque about Ryuji's tone, and it made Ginzo raise an eyebrow in Kosuke's direction.

"What do you think happened here?" he asked his young friend.

"Can't say… it's really not clear. But from first glance it seems that he was wounded over by the folding screen, and managed to escape as far as this genkan. Then he collapsed as he was trying to get the front door open. Did you see the screen?"

Ginzo and Kosuke returned to the larger tatami room. The screen was lying in the same position as it had been the night before, but now it had a vertical cut running from the top end about twelve inches down. The shiny gold leaf had more blood splashed on it, and in between spray marks that resembled a sprinkling of flower petals, there were partially dried fingerprints. Yet again, there were only three fingers, only this time as there were no traces of koto picks over the fingers, the swirls and whorl pattern of the prints were visible, albeit faintly. Ginzo grimaced, and then turned his attention to the koto which was lying by the screen. It had another broken string and missing bridge, but this time the bridge was lying next to the instrument.

"Kosuke, when you first arrived were the shutters—?"

"They were closed. I reached in through the hole made by the axe and undid the bolt. Take a look outside, over by the stone lantern."

Ginzo stepped onto the engawa floor and looked out through the open rain shutter. Just to the right of the stone lantern lay a katana. It gleamed dully in the morning mist.

There's no hiding anything in the countryside. News travels fast, and by daybreak the whole village had erupted with rumours that a second tragedy had befallen the Ichiyanagi family. News had spread to the surrounding villages too. But in the midst of the commotion there was one more piece of intelligence. This piece of news changed the face of the case completely…

That morning around nine o'clock a man came bicycling in from K— town, requesting an urgent meeting with the person in charge of the case. As Inspector Isokawa was also on his way to the scene of the latest crime, the two quickly found each other. I will record the man's statement here.

There is a female patient currently hospitalized at Kiuchi Hospital in K—. Yesterday, this woman was injured in an automobile accident that occurred in town, and was brought to the hospital, but this morning when she heard about the incident at the Ichiyanagi residence, she became agitated. She claims to know something about the case, and is anxious to meet with the person in charge. She says she knows who the killer is.

Kosuke was with the inspector when the man related the story, and grew excited as he listened. He was sure it was the same woman he'd seen—the one who'd been on the train from Kurashiki. The one who had attracted his attention, but whom he'd forgotten all about amid all the commotion surrounding the case.

"Inspector, I think we should go and talk to this woman. I'm convinced she knows something."

And so Inspector Isokawa and Kosuke Kindaichi set off together by bicycle for Kiuchi Hospital. The woman was indeed the same one that Kosuke had seen on the train. She lay on a thin mattress. her head and hand bandaged up, but she seemed to be in reasonable shape, considering all that she'd suffered.

"And would you be the officer in charge of this case?"

She spoke clearly and politely, and despite her horrific injuries she retained a particular sort of dignity, very probably from her training as a professional educator.

Isokawa confirmed that he was in charge, and she introduced herself as Shizuko Shiraki, a teacher at S— Girls' High

116

School in Osaka, and a close friend of the murdered bride, Katsuko Kubo.

"I see. And you say you have some information about the murder case?"

Shizuko nodded emphatically, and reached for her handbag. She produced two letters, and handed one of them to Inspector Isokawa.

"Please take a look at this."

It was a letter from Katsuko Kubo to Shizuko Shiraki, dated 20th October, or about a month earlier. The two men each took a deep breath, and began to read. This is an approximation of what I believe they read.

My Dear Shizuko

I'm writing to you first and foremost because I owe you an apology. You told me that before my wedding I must bury away my secret in the darkness. Bringing it to light is not the way to bring happiness to married life was what you warned me. But I have broken my promise to you, and have revealed the whole story of that hateful T— to Kenzo. But don't worry—I don't regret it one bit. Naturally, at first he was shocked, but in the end he showed the greatest compassion and forgave me. Of course this whole business—the fact that I'm not a virgin—must have hurt Kenzo greatly. But rather than keeping such a secret, and suffering from guilt throughout the whole of my married life, I feel it's so much better this way. This way I can embark on a happy married life from the outset. Whatever shadow I have cast over my husband's heart, now with all my greatest effort and affection I will show that I can erase the poor image that Kenzo has of me. So please, my dear friend, don't worry about me.

Your friend, Katsuko

As soon as Isokawa and Kosuke had finished reading the first letter, Shizuko handed them the second. This one was dated 16th November, nine days before the wedding.

Dear Shizuko

Please help! I'm in a state of panic. Yesterday I went with my Uncle Ginzo to Mitsukoshi Department Store in Osaka. (Please forgive me for not dropping by to see you—I couldn't really with my uncle there.) We were there to buy things for the wedding ceremony, but who do you think I ran into? It was T—. I was so horrified. Can you imagine? He's changed so much since those days. He's become so wild and degenerate. He was in the company of another youth who you could tell at a glance was some kind of gangster... I must have turned white at the sight of them. My heart seemed to turn to ice and my whole body started to tremble. Of course, I had no intention of saying a word to him. But then... but then T— waited until my uncle's attention was elsewhere and he approached me. With a horrible smirk on his face, he put his mouth right up to my ear and whispered, "Getting married, are you? Congratulations." I felt so shamed, so humiliated. Shizuko, what should I do? I'd never set eyes on him since that day we broke it off six years ago. I'd buried him deep in the past, or so I thought. I'd told Kenzo, and he'd forgiven me for that reason. The two of us had vowed never to speak T—'s name ever again. And then to bump into him now! Of course, that one incident in Mitsukoshi was all. After that T— left without a backward glance... But Shizu-chan, what should I do?

Yours, Katsuko

Inspector Isokawa finished reading and couldn't contain his excitement.

"Shiraki-san, do you mean that you believe this 'T—' to be the killer?"

"Yes, I think he must be. I can't imagine anyone more likely to have committed such a heinous crime."

Shizuko Shiraki spoke as if delivering a stern lecture to her pupils. She went on:

"T—'s real name is Shozo Taya. He's the son of a wealthy family from Suma in Kobe. When he first met Katsuko he was wearing the uniform of some medical university. Later it transpired that he wasn't a student at that university at all—he'd taken the entrance examination three times and failed each time. Katsuko was an intelligent young woman, but she fell prey to the same kind of predator that so many unsophisticated country girls newly alone in the city do. Taya completely took advantage of her.

"Katsuko didn't enter into a relationship with him lightly. She was in love, fully intending to marry him one day. But that dream barely lasted three months. As well as discovering that he wasn't really a medical student, she also learned of many dubious activities he was involved in. By the fourth month she decided she had to break it off. I was the one who went with her to help her do it, and he was totally brazen. He admitted everything: 'You found me out—well, never mind. I get it— it's over.' Still, his parting words were somewhat reassuring. He looked at Katsuko, who was in tears, and said, 'Kubo-san, don't worry, I won't be a burden to you any longer.' And after that, as Katsuko wrote in that letter, she never saw Taya again, never even heard talk of him.

"However, I have to admit that I heard rumours from time

119

to time: that he'd gone bad, that he was sleeping around, and eventually joined the yakuza. I even heard he was into extortion and blackmail. That's the kind of man that Katsuko was once romantically involved with. I'm convinced that when he heard that she was getting married, he couldn't stand it. I'm sure that it was Taya who killed Katsuko and her husband."

Kosuke listened enthralled, and waited for Shizuko to finish. Then he pulled out a photograph and showed it to her. It was, of course, the one that Inspector Isokawa had given to him the previous day, the "mortal enemy" from Kenzo's photograph album.

"Shiraki-san, is the man in this photograph Taya?"

Surprised, Shizuko reached out and took the picture, but immediately shook her head.

"No," she said firmly. "That's not him. Taya is far more handsome."

CHAPTER 12

The Grave Is Opened

Shizuko Shiraki's story had a remarkable impact on Kosuke Kindaichi and Inspector Isokawa. Although they each took away a different impression from it, within the story was the key to solving the case. However, neither of them would completely understand that until later.

For now, Kosuke and Isokawa left Kiuchi Hospital deep in thought. Although they were considering the exact same set of circumstances, their expressions were poles apart. Inspector Isokawa looked as if he'd swallowed a very bitter-tasting bug, but Kosuke Kindaichi looked bizarrely cheerful. In fact, he looked positively thrilled as he rode back, one hand on the bicycle handlebar and the other scratching his scalp through his wind-blown tangle of hair.

The two cycled through the town in silence following the river, and were approaching the turning for the road that led back to O— village when all of a sudden Kosuke shouted to Isokawa to stop.

"Ju-just a minute. Wait a moment."

Puzzled, Inspector Isokawa got off his bicycle and followed Kosuke into a tobacconist's on the street corner. Kosuke ordered a pack of Cherry Brand cigarettes.

"Excuse me," he asked the shopkeeper. "Does the road branching off over there lead to H— village?"

"Yes, it does."

"So I take that road and then what's the rest of the route? Is it obvious?"

"Yes, pretty much. If you go straight along that road, you come to O— village. There's a local government office there. Ask there for directions to the Ichiyanagi place in Yamanoya. It's a big old mansion—you can't miss it. Take the road that runs by the Ichiyanagi front gate. The road takes you up over the hills but it's a straight run, so there's no chance of getting lost."

Absorbed in her knitting, the shopkeeper barely glanced up.

"I see. Thank you very much."

Kosuke's expression was jubilant as they left the tobacconist's. Isokawa stared at him in bewilderment, but Kosuke made no move to explain.

"Sorry for the hold-up," he said, jumping back on his bicycle. "Shall we go?"

Isokawa thought about Kosuke's question, but he couldn't for the life of him work out why he'd asked it. Still uncomprehending, he followed Kosuke through O— village, and into the tiny hamlet of Yamanoya, back to the Ichiyanagi residence.

While the two detectives had been away, Saburo had been moved to the main house and was being attended to by Ryuji and the village physician, Doctor F—. His wound was deep, and he seemed to have contracted tetanus from the injury. At one point he had been in a critical condition, but by the time Isokawa and Kosuke pulled up on their bicycles, there had been a slight improvement and it seemed he might be able to withstand some questioning. Isokawa immediately rushed into the sickroom, but surprisingly Kosuke made no attempt to join them. Instead he dismounted and hurried over to talk to Detective Sergeant Kimura and another young police detective who happened to be in the vicinity. They both looked amazed by what he had to say.

"Really? You want us to go to H— village right now?"

"Right. Right. Sorry for the trouble, but could you go house to house and perform a thorough search? I don't imagine there can be that many homes."

"Yes, that's true but… What about the inspector?"

"Don't worry. I'll explain everything to Inspector Isokawa. This is an extremely important matter. Now, let me give you this…"

Kosuke handed Sergeant Kimura the photo of the three-fingered man that he had shown to Shizuko Shiraki. Kimura put it away in his pocket, then, both still looking rather perplexed, the detectives hopped on their bicycles and cycled off at full speed. Kosuke watched them leave then headed into the main house. Ginzo was waiting for him just inside.

"Kosuke, don't you want to hear what Saburo has to say?"

"No, it's fine. Anyway, I can always hear it from the inspector afterwards."

"You've sent the detectives to H— village. Is there something there?"

"Yes, well… I'll tell you about that later."

Ginzo looked hard into his friend's eyes and exhaled deeply.

He understood. Kosuke was no longer fumbling in the dark. Inside his brain—that replacement for a magnifying glass and tape measure—the building blocks of logic and reasoning were right now being fitted together one by one. The twinkle in his eye gave it away. He had almost solved the puzzle.

"You learned something in K— town, didn't you?"

"Yes, I need to talk to you about that, but not right here. Let's go inside."

123

They went into the sitting room. No one was there; conveniently for Kosuke and Ginzo, the whole Ichiyanagi family was at Saburo's bedside.

What Kosuke needed to say to Ginzo was extremely painful for him to express. He knew Ginzo had loved Katsuko deeply, had trusted her implicitly, and to reveal her secret now was going to cause his friend great distress. But there was no way around it—he had to tell Ginzo what he'd discovered.

The older man was as shocked as Kosuke knew he would be. He looked absolutely wretched, like a dog that had been beaten.

"Ko-san, this can't… I mean… is it true?"

"I believe it is. There's no reason for this woman to come all this way to tell us a lie. And I saw the letter that Katsuko wrote."

"But why didn't Katsuko tell me about it? Why did she confide in this friend?…"

"Uncle?"

Kosuke gave Ginzo's shoulder a sympathetic squeeze.

"Girls generally don't confide in their parents or their closest relatives. It's much easier for them to open up to their friends."

"Huh."

Ginzo sat for a while looking utterly dejected, but this was an energetic man with only one purpose, one concern in the world, and he couldn't stay down for long. Presently, his spirit seemed to return to him, and he lifted his head.

"And so?… What does this mean? Is this man 'T—'—Shozo Taya—the murderer?"

"That's what Inspector Isokawa believes, and it's what the woman Shizuko Shiraki claims."

"So Taya is the three-fingered man?"

"Actually, he isn't. I thought he might be, so that's why I showed the photo to Shizuko, but she was positive that it wasn't the same man. The inspector is rather upset that the lead turned out to be a dead end."

Kosuke's eyes crinkled. Ginzo looked at him suspiciously.

"So, Ko-san, what do you think about it? It seems to me that you don't believe this Taya character had anything to do with the murders."

"No, on the contrary. I believe that he had a huge connection to the case— Oh, can I help you?"

Kiyo, the maid, was looking in through the gap in the shoji doors.

"Pardon me, I thought the young lady of the house might be in here," said Kiyo, ready to make a hurried retreat.

"No, we haven't seen Suzuko-san. Oh, just a minute, Kiyo-san?"

"Yes, sir?"

"There's something I'd like to check with you. That night, after the wedding, who was present at the final sake cup ceremony in the annexe house? There was the village mayor, the bride and groom, and the mother of the groom. Then of course Ryosuke and Akiko?"

"That's correct. Nobody else."

"And I believe that evening the lady dowager was wearing a kimono bearing the family crest. Were you the one to fold and put it away afterwards?"

Kiyo was clearly very surprised by the question.

"No, I didn't put it away."

"So who did?"

"Nobody put it away. Her ladyship is very particular about her clothes. She never lets anybody touch her kimonos. She always folds them herself. But with what happened that night she hasn't had the time to do it properly. It's still hanging in her room back there."

Kosuke leapt to his feet.

"C-c-could you take me to th-that room now?"

His enthusiasm was so intense that Kiyo was startled. She took several steps backwards and looked as if she were about to burst into tears. Ginzo, who was also surprised by Kosuke's reaction, tried to soothe her.

"Kiyo-san, don't be alarmed. I'll go along too. So which is Itoko-san's room?"

"This way, please."

The two followed Kiyo and as they walked Ginzo whispered to the young detective:

"Ko-san, what is it? Is there something significant about Itoko-san's kimono?"

Kosuke nodded emphatically several times. He didn't trust himself to try speaking again. He knew his stammer would come back.

Just as Kiyo had said, the family-crest kimono was on a bamboo clothes hanger, which was suspended from a beam in the bedroom. Kosuke began to feel around both of its concealed sleeve pockets until suddenly his face lit up.

"Ki-Kiyo-san, you can go now," he said, grinning.

Kiyo threw him one more uneasy look and left the room. Kosuke watched her go and then reached into the sleeve pocket.

"Uncle, the secret of the trick has been revealed. You know that one where the conjurer on the stage drops a wristwatch into a magic box and the watch disappears, eventually turning up in the pocket of someone in the audience? Everyone's seen that trick done. The audience member has been planted and has had an identical watch in his pocket since the start of the show. The solution is that there are two watches, and the challenge for the conjurer lies in pretending to put the first watch into the box while managing to conceal it somewhere else. And look, here it is—that first watch!"

Kosuke pulled his hand from the kimono sleeve pocket, and held it out for Ginzo to see. There in his palm lay a koto bridge, engraved with a bird on a wave.

"Ko-san! Is that—?" Ginzo gasped.

Kosuke continued to grin.

"Like I said, Uncle, this is the key to the trick. The big reveal, and yet still only the beginning. That night— Oh, hello there. Come on in."

Ginzo turned towards the engawa, where a timid-looking Suzuko had just appeared, dressed in a long-sleeved kimono.

"Perfect timing, Suzu-chan," he said warmly. "We hope you can answer a question for us. Is this a bridge from the Lovebird koto?"

Suzuko nervously entered the room. She took a look at the item in Kosuke's hand, and nodded.

"There was already a bridge missing from the koto before you played it at the wedding, wasn't there?" said Kosuke. "Do you know when that bridge went missing?"

"I don't know exactly. It was gone when I got the koto out."

"And when did you get it out?"

"The day the bride arrived. That morning I got it out of the storehouse. I saw there was one bridge missing so I took one off my practice koto and put it on the Lovebird."

"So the koto was kept in the storehouse. Could anyone go in and out of this storehouse?"

"No, usually it's not open. But because the bride was coming we needed loads of stuff out of it, so it had been open for a while."

"I see. So lots of people were going in and out?"

"Yes, everybody was going in and out. They needed plates and bowls and *zabuton* cushions and folding screens. They had to get them all out of the storehouse."

"Thank you. You're a smart girl, aren't you, Suzu-chan? By the way—"

Kosuke put a gentle hand on her shoulder and looked into her childlike face.

"Suzu-chan, why are you so worried about your dead cat?"

Later Kosuke Kindaichi would say he had no idea this question would turn out to be so significant. He was just curious to discover what distressing secret a simple girl was holding in her heart that would cause her to go roaming at night around the grave of her dead pet.

However, the question seemed to terrify Suzuko. Her expression immediately clouded over.

"Tama?…"

"Yes, Tama. Do you remember doing anything bad to Tama?"

"No, no. Of course I didn't."

"Then why are you so upset?… Suzu-chan, when did Tama die?"

"The day before the wedding. He died early in the morning."

"I see. And then the next morning you held his funeral. Is that right?"

Suzuko didn't reply. But then all of a sudden, she burst into tears. Kosuke and Ginzo exchanged a look but then Kosuke suddenly seemed to have remembered something and his breathing quickened.

"Suzu-chan, is it possible that you didn't hold Tama's funeral on the morning of the wedding ceremony? Have you been telling a lie?"

Suzuko began to cry even harder.

"I'm sorry. I'm sorry. But I felt sorry for poor Tama. Going in a cold grave all alone. Poor Tama. So I put him in his box and hid it inside a closet, and then… my big brother was killed."

"Hm. Your big brother was killed… And then?"

"I got really scared. Because Sabu-chan told me that if you leave a dead cat lying around, it'll turn into a ghost. He threatened me saying that something bad would happen. So I got scared and while everybody was all upset about Kenzo dying, I went and buried Tama."

That was Suzuko's secret. The one that had been haunting her so badly that she had started sleepwalking.

"So Suzu-chan, the box that you put Tama into, the coffin— during the wedding ceremony and when that terrible thing happened to your big brother, it was in your room the whole time?"

"I'm sorry. I'm really sorry. If I'd told my mother, she'd have been so angry with me."

"Uncle!"

Kosuke suddenly jumped up and moved away from Suzuko, as if something had just occurred to him.

"Never mind, Suzu-chan," said Ginzo kindly. "It's all right. You told the truth and now there's nothing more to worry about. Come on, dry your tears and go back to the others. Kiyo-san's been looking for you, you know."

Wiping her eyes as she went, Suzuko scurried out onto the engawa. Kosuke listened a moment to the pitter-patter of her footsteps, then grabbed Ginzo by the arm.

"Uncle, let's go and look. We have to check the cat's grave."

"Ko-san, what are you—?"

But Kosuke wasn't listening. Holding up the hem of his worn-out old hakama, he shot off towards the front door, Ginzo of course rushing to keep up.

They went straight to the end of the garden where the grave was located. As luck would have it, the shovel that had been used to dig up the grave the previous day was still lying there. Kosuke seized it and began to dig.

"Ko-san, why on earth are you—?"

"That girl's naive lie had me completely blinkered. At the time of the murders, the cat's coffin was still in Suzuko's room."

"You're saying the killer hid something inside? But we just dug up this grave yesterday."

"Y-yes. But th-that means afterwards would be the safest time to hide something in it."

It took no time at all to dig down to the wooden box. Its lid had been pried off just a day earlier, so the nails were already loose, and this time it was easy to remove. Inside it looked just as before. The tender-hearted Suzuko had wrapped the tiny body of the kitten in a silken blanket.

Kosuke took a stick and used it to poke open the blanket, then reached down and with one finger and thumb carefully extracted something from underneath—a parcel wrapped in oilpaper and tied up with string. It was about the same size as the kitten.

Ginzo was amazed. The parcel definitely hadn't been there in the coffin when they'd checked the day before.

Kosuke tore off a corner of the oilpaper and peered inside. Then he immediately held it up for Ginzo to see.

"L-L-Look, Uncle. It w-was here after all."

Ginzo looked through the tear in the oilpaper, and all at once the ground seemed to sway under his feet. In all his years on this earth he never had and never would again experience a shock like this one. Even though in this case alone there were still many more grisly discoveries to come, nothing would come close to the sheer horror of this moment.

CHAPTER 13

Inspector Isokawa is Shaken

"Hey, where have you two been?"

Inspector Isokawa was sitting on the veranda of the main building, watching Kosuke and Ginzo walk back from their visit to the cat's grave.

"Just went for a walk."

"A walk? Around the garden?"

"Yep, that's right."

Isokawa looked the two men up and down. Ginzo's ashen face was unmissable.

"What's wrong? Did something happen?"

"No, what do you mean? We're fine."

"Seriously. What have you got there?"

"Oh, this?"

Hanging from Kosuke's hand was an object wrapped in a bundle inside a large handkerchief. He swung it nonchalantly.

"A souvenir," he announced, a grin on his face.

"Souvenir?"

"Right. But, Inspector, perhaps you shouldn't ask so many questions. How about a few answers? What's happened with Saburo?"

"Yes, well… I think you'd better sit down. Kubo-san, are you feeling all right? You're looking very pale…"

"What? Oh, we've been talking about Katsuko's murder; of

course he's feeling miserable right now. So, what did Saburo tell you?"

"Well, he was rambling rather, but I really think that this time you have to share the blame, Kindaichi-san."

"You're joking! Me? How on—?"

"Yesterday you were having a heated discussion with Saburo about detective novels. Well, it seems that provoked him. You were talking about locked room murders, weren't you? Saburo decided to try to solve this locked room case himself, so last night he sneaked into the annexe house."

"I see. So that's what he— Anyway, what then?"

"Well, he locked all the doors completely from the inside. In other words, he was trying to recreate the conditions exactly as they were the night of the murders. But as he was doing that, he got the feeling that there was someone in the closet behind the tokonoma alcove. There wasn't really any noise; it was just a feeling. He thought he could hear someone breathing. So eventually he couldn't help it—he had to go and take a look. So..."

"Yes, yes. So he?..."

"So Saburo opened the closet door and a man jumped out, brandishing a sword. Of course, Saburo screamed and tried to run away, but he only got as far as the large tatami room before his shoulder and the screen were sliced open. After that he was in a daze and he doesn't remember any more. He doesn't even recall making his way to the genkan door."

"I see. And what did this attacker look like?"

"He only got a glimpse of him as it was dark, and on top of that he was startled, so he says he didn't get a proper look at his face. I think that's very likely under the circumstances.

133

But he did say that he appeared to be wearing an oversized surgical mask... Well, that's about it."

"I suppose he didn't get a look at the man's fingers either, then?"

"Of course not. He didn't have time to check something like that. However, from the bloody fingerprints left behind I think we can conclude that it was none other than the three-fingered man for sure."

Kosuke and Ginzo exchanged glances.

"And then?... Was that all Saburo had to say?"

"Well, yes. That was about it. I'd really hoped to hear a more precise account, but I was disappointed. Kindaichi-san, this case is really beginning to weigh heavily on me. There's this other man, Taya, to deal with too. I can't even tell whether he has any connection to the three-fingered man. It makes my damn head ache."

"Come on, please don't take it so hard. There'll be some good news any time now." Kosuke got to his feet. "I'd forgotten all about it, but the detective that was here before, what's-his-name, I sent him off to H— village."

"You mean Kimura? What business did you have for him in H—?"

"There was something I needed him to look into for me. Anyway, Uncle, shall we be going?"

"Where are you two off to?"

It sounded almost like a challenge.

"Oh, just for a walk. We're going to take a little stroll over that way. Inspector, you'll be here for a while, will you?"

Isokawa looked suspiciously at Kosuke.

"So if you are," Kosuke continued blithely, "would you mind asking Ryuji-san something for me? He claims to have arrived here on the morning after the murders. However, just after midday the day before—in other words on the 25th, the day of the wedding—he was seen getting off a train at N— station. The witness appears to be telling the truth. Would you mind asking Ryuji-san why he lied to us?"

"Wh-what did you say?" Isokawa stammered.

"Now, now, Inspector. There really is no call to impersonate me. Uncle, let's go."

With that, Kosuke and Ginzo left the inspector sitting on the veranda, dumbstruck. They made their way around the house to the back gate.

This back gate was on the west side of the property and was where the mysterious three-fingered man had apparently entered the grounds on the day of the wedding. The two men went through it and found themselves at the stream that ran along the west side of the residence. They followed the path that ran along the riverbank towards the north.

"Ko-san, where are we going?"

"I'm not sure. But the dog that trots around finds the bone. Let's try trotting around this area."

Kosuke's handkerchief-wrapped bundle still swung from his hand.

They followed the stream in a northerly direction until they reached the mill with its waterwheel. The wheel was not currently turning.

Right after the bridge by the mill, the path became extra narrow, made a sharp bend to the east and began to climb up the cliff edge. Kosuke and Ginzo rounded the bend and came face to face with a sizeable pond.

This part of Okayama Prefecture was famous for its rice cultivation, and many ponds had been created for irrigation purposes, so this kind of feature was not at all unusual. However, at the sight of this particular pond, Kosuke stopped dead and stared into its depths. Then he called out to a passing farmhand:

"Excuse me, do you drain this pond every year?"

"Yes, we do."

"Has it already been done this year?"

"No, not yet… It's meant to be done every 25th of November but this year—well, what with everyone busy helping with the big event at the Ichiyanagi place—it got put off until the 5th of next month."

Kosuke looked disappointed.

"Ah, I see. And the Ichiyanagi family knows about this of course?"

"Yes, they know. This pond was dug by the old head of the family, Sakue-san. So whenever we're going to drain it, we go and ask permission at the Ichiyanagi house. No real meaning to it, but it's become the custom."

"I see. Thank you."

They left the farmhand behind and continued up the path along the cliff edge. Ginzo didn't ask, but it was clear that Kosuke knew exactly what he was looking for, so Ginzo just followed silently behind. After a while, there was a visible curve in the line of the cliff edge up ahead.

"Ah! There it is," Kosuke called out as they arrived at the curve in the path. Just beyond, there was a narrow patch of flat land, and on it was a small semi-cylindrical structure made from clay, just over twenty square feet in size. It was a charcoal kiln.

There were no professional charcoal makers out there in the country. The local folks were quite canny at saving money and would make charcoal for their own personal use. Farmers would construct their own kiln from bricks and clay. Each one was built on a very small scale; it could manage no more than six or seven bags at a time, or at the most about twelve. A typical kiln was scarcely bigger than this one, and height-wise came up to about chest-level on a man.

Kosuke and Ginzo had come across one of these kilns. From the carbonized stick that was protruding from it, it seemed that someone had just finished making a batch of charcoal. Kosuke ran over and bent down to peer in through the narrow opening. Inside was a man with a handkerchief wrapped around his head, down on his hands and knees, scraping up the fragments of charcoal. It looked as if he had almost got all the pieces out.

"Hey, there!"

At the sound of Kosuke's voice, the man stopped and looked around.

"I have a question for you. Could you come out a moment?"

The man continued to rummage in the kiln awhile, but eventually emerged, still on all-fours. He brought with him two bamboo baskets filled with charcoal. The man's face and hands were black with ash; his eyes two bright points in the middle.

"What do you want?"

"When did you light the fire to make this batch of charcoal? It's a very important question, so please answer truthfully."

In the countryside whenever something unusual happens, news spreads very quickly. It had been common knowledge since the previous day that this short, unremarkable youth in the shabby hakama was a famous detective from the city. The farmer, slightly flustered by the appearance of the famous

137

detective at his charcoal kiln, began to count on his knobbly fingers.

"Let's see. I must have lit the furnace on the evening of the 25th. Yes, without a doubt. It was the day of the Ichiyanagi wedding."

"And the wood? When did you put that in?"

"Hmm, yes, the timber. I put that in the day before—so the 24th. But I'd only got about half of it done before nightfall, so I went home. Then the following evening I stuffed in the rest of the branches and lit the furnace."

"Between the two visits did you notice anything had changed? Anything that struck you as strange?"

"Now that you mention it, after I set the fire on the evening of the 25th, I came back later that night from time to time to check on it. Yes, that was it—definitely the 25th—it was snowing heavily. Anyway, I could have sworn there was a strange smell coming from the kiln. A foul stink like burning skin. I thought a dead cat or something had got mixed up with the firewood, but no, someone had been playing a prank. They'd stuck some dirty old clothes and a pair of shoes in through the chimney. See, I pulled them out."

The pile of clothes he indicated was burnt beyond recognition, but despite having turned completely black, the shoes had kept their shape. Kosuke poked at them with a stick.

"May I take a look inside the kiln?"

"Yes, but there's nothing left in there."

Oblivious to his hakama trailing in the charcoal ash, Kosuke stooped down and entered the kiln. He could be heard scrabbling about in the darkness awhile before emitting a wild shriek.

"Q-quick! C-come here!"

"Y-yes?" said the charcoal maker, running to the kiln entrance.

"Hahaha! Everyone's impersonating me today... Please, could you run down to the Ichiyanagi place and get the police inspector to come up here right away? If any of the local police or our detectives are there too, could you have them join him? Oh, and get them to bring some shovels with them too."

"Wh-what shall I tell them—?"

"They'll find out soon enough. But please hurry!"

After the man had shot off like a pitch-black pebble thrown from the cliff, Kosuke emerged from the kiln, the tip of his own nose covered in soot.

"Ko-san, inside that kiln, is it?…"

Kosuke nodded briefly, confirming Ginzo's suspicions. He gulped and didn't ask anything further. Kosuke also kept silent. Above them in the late autumn sky, they could hear birds singing.

After a while, Inspector Isokawa turned up with one of his junior detectives and a local police constable, the latter two with shovels in their hands. They were all slightly out of breath and very curious.

"Kindaichi-san, what's going on?"

"Inspector, please dig up the ground in the bottom of this kiln. There's a corpse buried underneath."

"A c-corpse?" bleated the charcoal maker, sounding exactly like an injured goat.

The police constable and the young detective paid him no attention. They made for the entrance of the kiln, but Ginzo stopped them.

"Just a minute. I don't think you'll be able to dig like that."

He turned to address the charcoal maker.

"This is your kiln, isn't it?"

"Er… yes."

"Right then, of course we'll reimburse you later, but this outer shell will have to be knocked down."

By shell, he meant the roof of the kiln.

"Well, I, er… I don't mind, but a corpse? A corpse in there? That's crazy."

The charcoal maker looked as if he were about to burst into tears any moment. The constable and the junior detective set about bashing in the semi-cylindrical roof of the kiln. It was a simple structure, built by a layman out of clay, so it didn't prove difficult. As soon as the hole was large enough for the interior to be filled with light, the two law officers jumped down into the interior. As Inspector Isokawa, Kosuke and Ginzo watched from above, they began to dig.

It wasn't long before part of a man's leg became visible, one that had turned a grotesque colour.

"Ugh! It's naked," said the junior detective in disgust.

"Kindaichi-san! Who is this? Does it have something to do with this case?" asked Isokawa.

"Hmm. Never mind that for now. You'll soon see."

The body was lying on its back. The policemen gradually exposed its emaciated belly, then worked upwards to its chest area. At that point, the detective let out another cry.

"Argh! He was murdered all right. Look at the chest. There's a huge stab wound in it."

"Wh-what the—?"

This time it was Kosuke's turn to be startled. He literally jumped in the air.

"Ko-san," asked Inspector Isokawa, "surely you can't be surprised that this man was murdered?"

"I-I-I— No, no, but…"

"Hurry up, you two, and dig up the face!"

At Inspector Isokawa's command, the policemen began to dig in the region of the corpse's head, and the detective called out for a third time.

"Inspector, it's him. That man. See, this great long scar on his face? It's the three-fingered man!"

"What are you talking about?"

Isokawa craned his neck to look at the corpse's face, and his eyes almost popped out of his skull. There was no mistake—there lay the indescribably revolting face of the dead man with a long, stitched-up wound running from the right-hand corner of his top lip up his right cheek. Just as if his mouth had been split open.

"Kindaichi-san, this is— This can't be— Hey, you two! Dig up his hand, his right hand."

They dug but this time all three—the junior detective, the police constable and Inspector Isokawa—let out a scream. The corpse had no right hand. It had been completely severed at the wrist.

"Kindaichi-san!"

"Don't worry, Inspector. Don't worry. This all makes sense. Here. Your souvenir."

Isokawa fixed Kosuke so hard with his bloodshot eyes that it seemed he was trying to bore a hole into his face. Eventually those eyes dropped to the handkerchief-wrapped bundle that Kosuke had handed him.

"Open it up. I found it in the cat's grave."

There was no doubt that Inspector Isokawa had worked out by the feel of the package exactly what it contained. He took a deep breath and with trembling fingers undid the

141

handkerchief, cut the string and opened up the oilpaper. Inside was a man's right hand, severed at the wrist. It had only three fingers: the thumb, index finger and middle finger.

"Inspector, this is the stamp used to make all those bloody fingerprints."

CHAPTER 14

Kosuke's Experiment

That evening Kosuke Kindaichi solved this most bizarre of murder cases by way of an intriguing experiment.

Kosuke issued a special invitation to Doctor F— asking for his assistance. The doctor made detailed notes on the events of the evening, so I am going to borrow these to tell my story. From other sections of these notes, it is clear that this doctor was generally, due to the nature of his job, a calm character, not easily perturbed, but on this particular occasion his notes reveal that he was astounded by the events that transpired. I will do my best to edit out much of the doctor's personal reactions, and to relate the information to you in as matter-of-fact a style as possible. I do believe that is what befits the conclusion of this case. And so, without further ado, I present the following section in the voice of Dr F—.

(AN EXCERPT FROM DOCTOR F—'S NOTES)

I received notice from that curious young man, Kosuke Kindaichi, that he was planning to perform an experiment that night at the Ichiyanagi residence. It was shortly after the ghastly corpse of the three-fingered man had been dug up.

I'd performed an autopsy on the body right away. When I'd finished, Kindaichi-san had a request for me.

"Whatever you've discovered about this body, no matter how strange, could you refrain from releasing it until I've finished my little experiment?"

I was surprised by his request. I had indeed found something totally unexpected during my autopsy. However, at the time I had no idea why he didn't want me to reveal my findings. It wasn't until much later that evening that I would understand.

Still, I couldn't help but be filled with admiration for this young man with the mysterious, almost magical powers of insight and observation. From what I'd heard the police hadn't just happened to come across the corpse; Kindaichi-san had directed them to exactly where to dig. He must have known that the three-fingered man was dead, and where he was buried. And then, in addition, he must have already realized the strange truth that would emerge as a result of my autopsy. This young detective with his ungainly manner, wild, dishevelled hair and stammer had become to my eye something of a genius. I didn't even hesitate to do as he requested. I was in a state of great anticipation and looking forward to observing this experiment.

This is how the evening unfolded.

As agreed, I arrived at the Ichiyanagi residence around 9 p.m. and was directed to the annexe house. Detective Sergeant Kimura was on duty at the garden gate that separated it from the rest of the residence but he left his post to accompany me to the front door. All of the amado shutters were closed, but after Sergeant Kimura showed me into the famous tatami room, I found there were already four men assembled, seated around a charcoal brazier, quietly smoking. The four were Kosuke Kindaichi, Inspector Isokawa, Ginzo Kubo and finally, the sole representative of the family, Ryuji Ichiyanagi. Seeing

144

how pale and nervous everyone looked, I couldn't help sensing that we had arrived at the final scene of this drama.

Seeing me approach, Kindaichi-san quickly disposed of his cigarette butt in the brazier.

"Well then, we're all assembled. It's time to begin the experiment."

He sprung to his feet.

"Now, as the original crime took place around four in the morning, technically we're rather early for beginning the experiment, but I don't want to keep everyone waiting around, so let's get things underway. The early start does mean there will be several artificial aspects to our re-enactment. This is unavoidable and I apologize to you all in advance."

He put two fingers into his mouth and whistled. Immediately there was the sound of footsteps—someone outside running from the east to the west end of the annexe house. We were all startled, but Kindaichi-san just smiled.

"What's the matter? That's just Sergeant Kimura. I asked him to take care of the artificial aspect I just mentioned."

Kindaichi-san went over to the byobu folding screen that had been placed in front of the tokonoma alcove and moved it aside. Everyone murmured in surprise. Behind it stood a life-sized straw doll.

"I got the local farmhand, Genshichi, to make it for me. To be accurate, there were two people in the room on the night of the murder, but for the purposes of this experiment, just one will do. Otherwise, I'd like you all to check that the room is in the exact same state it was that night. The amount that the west-side shoji sliding door was open for example… And this screen, is it in the right position? The bodies were found on this side, is that right?"

With Inspector Isokawa's help, Kindaichi-san moved the folding screen over to where it had stood the night of the murders. Suddenly he made a sign as if to shush us. At first, I didn't understand why, but then as it fell quiet in the room, I could make out the sound of the waterwheel turning. It had only just started up and its steady creak created a distinct background noise. We looked at each other.

"Sergeant Kimura has opened the water channel for us. As you probably know already, that waterwheel doesn't turn constantly. The water channel is normally blocked off. When it's needed, they open the channel and the flowing water causes the waterwheel to turn. But recently Shokichi, who is in charge of hulling the rice, is too busy with other farm work in the daytime, so he comes around four in the morning to start up the mill. In other words, every morning at 4 a.m. that waterwheel begins turning."

Kindaichi-san threw out all this information at high speed, as he dashed out into the engawa corridor and returned right away carrying an unsheathed katana sword in one hand and with the other pulling two lengths of some kind of cord, which seemed to be attached somewhere out of view behind him.

"This katana is the one that was hidden in the closet behind the tokonoma alcove. And this length of cord… see? It's koto string."

He pulled what had first looked to be two lengths of string in from the engawa, over the top of the folding screen and into the main part of the room. But now that I looked again, there weren't two strings at all, but one single loop. Kindaichi-san took the end of this loop and slipped it over the hilt of the sword, wrapping it around a couple of extra times and tightening it just under the guard.

"Inspector, would you mind? The doll…"

Inspector Isokawa brought the straw doll over to Kindaichi-san, who was now standing just in front of the folding screen. We all watched spellbound, as with the hilt of the sword still in his right hand, Kindaichi-san took the doll in his left.

At the start of the experiment, the loop of koto string had been slack, hanging loosely over the top of the screen, but now we saw that it was being pulled away from us, as if someone were standing behind the screen, tugging it steadily towards them. Ginzo-san's eyes suddenly widened.

"Oh— the waterwheel!"

At that moment the koto string snapped tight. The guard on the sword was already up to the level of the top of the screen. Instantly, Kindaichi-san pushed the straw doll against the sword, plunging the tip into the doll's breast.

"Ah—!"

Inspector Isokawa, Ginzo-san, Ryuji-san all sat there, teeth and fists clenched, as they watched this grim re-enactment.

At the perfect moment, Kindaichi-san let go of the sword and the straw doll. The latter fell to the floor, and for a few moments the sword remained suspended at the top of the screen before ducking behind it. The next moment, the hilt of the sword clattered against the rain shutter behind.

We all ran into the west-side engawa. The double koto string was hanging through the ranma transom. With each turn of the waterwheel, it was being steadily pulled out through the gap between the decorative tree trunk and the door lintel. The sword was being pulled upwards by the string and for a few moments its guard became stuck in the corner of the transom. After a few more tugs on the string, the guard finally slipped through the gap, and the blade followed. At the same instant something fell from the transom with a soft thud. Kindaichi-san picked it up and showed it to Ginzo-san.

"Look. This is a hand towel like the one you found lying on the engawa when you broke in that night. It was draped over part of the transom to protect it from damage by the sword."

Kindaichi-san opened the rain shutters and we all rushed out into the garden, not a single one of us caring that we were barefoot outdoors in winter.

The moon had just risen so the garden was not terribly dark. The sword was there in front of us, dangling loosely in the air. The string wrapped around the guard now headed in two different directions—the line to the left running through the top of the stone lantern and heading off towards the north-west; the other line running back towards the roof of the annexe house. Kindaichi-san shone a flashlight in that direction, eliciting a cry from Inspector Isokawa.

"Ah! The koto bridge!"

Right at the corner of the protruding lavatory roof, some-one had attached a koto bridge, as a support for the koto string. As the waterwheel turned, the string was being reeled in until eventually the length of string between the koto bridge on the roof and the stone lantern grew taut. And the sword that hung right in the middle—

"There's the power of the waterwheel, and the two supports of the lantern and the koto bridge," explained Kosuke. "The weakest of the three points is bound to give."

A grating sound came from the direction of the waterwheel and the tension on the koto string kept increasing until with a pop the koto bridge flew from its perch on the roof and the string dropped loose.

"Inspector, try to find that bridge. I think it probably fell into the pile of leaves."

The inspector found it right away just next to the leaf pile.

All this while, the loosened string was tightening again. This time Kindaichi-san raised his flashlight and illuminated the trunk of the camphor tree.

"The sickle…"

Sure enough, there in the shade of the leaves was the sickle, driven into the trunk of the tree, and the koto string ran straight through the space between its freshly sharpened blade and the tree trunk. Kindaichi-san shone his flashlight into the space beyond the camphor tree.

"Watch the string on the far side," he said.

The string that ran over the blade of the sickle continued in a north-westerly direction. As the strain on it increased, several of the bamboo trees that hung over the edge of the cliff beyond were being bent lower and lower. Eventually there was one straight, taut line of string between the sickle and the top of the stone lantern. The sword was still hanging there in between, but now it was much closer to the lantern than before.

"This time we are comparing not only the power of the waterwheel with the stability of the the stone lantern and the sickle—we're adding one more element: the strength of the string. Of those four, which do you think is the weakest?"

And then it happened. As if in response, the bamboo trees suddenly sprang back and the string vibrated with a pinging sound. The part of the string that ran through the camphor tree was instantly severed by the sickle. A loud *twang zwing zwing* echoed through the air. The sword was tossed upwards, spun for a few moments, then thrust itself into the ground at the foot of the stone lantern.

"How about that, Uncle? Isn't that just about the same spot you found the sword stuck in the ground that night?"

But no one could reply. All that could be heard in the darkness was our ragged, heavy breathing. All eyes were on the sword, which was still vibrating in the ground.

"Right then, shall we take this opportunity to go and check where the string ended up?"

We looked up as if we'd only just realized Kindaichi-san was speaking to us. Then, one by one, we filed past the sword in the ground, and headed deep into the garden away from the annexe house. We followed the two ends of the severed string; both were being dragged from branch to branch and moving away steadily further into the distance. Eventually both ends of the string ended up at a large pine tree with a supported branch, and disappeared inside one of the bamboo supports.

"I think this is as far as we need to go. After this, the string passes through the hollowed-out bamboo and is tied around the axle of the waterwheel beyond. At the point where it meets the wheel, it's concealed by a length of thick rope, so that nobody would have noticed there was koto string there at all."

Ginzo-san let out a loud sigh. The inspector clicked his tongue and swore. Then we all returned to the rain-shuttered house. But right as we got there, Ryuji-san stopped dead and looked up.

"But the koto bridge…" he mumbled. "What was the point of it?"

"Ah, that was to make sure the sword wasn't dragged along the ground. Take a look—there's slightly too much distance between the camphor tree and this transom. So the perpetrator constructed something that would hold the load, and prevent the sword from leaving tracks in the snow. The person who constructed this whole device really didn't want that to happen. And it wasn't only the koto bridge. The byobu folding screen, the bamboo crutch, they were all cleverly used to support the string so that there were no traces left on the tatami matting or the ground. The screen, the sickle, the stone lantern, the bamboo, they were all things that were on hand, all things that wouldn't be out of place in the crime scene. It really offers us a glimpse of the brilliance of the designer, don't you think? The only unnatural element was the koto bridge. But instead, its use helped to make the whole case seem more mysterious. Clearly not a person of mediocre skill."

That was the end of the experiment. We all returned to that eight-tatami room. Back in the light, we saw Kindaichi-san's face was the only one that wasn't completely drained of colour.

CHAPTER 15

The Tragedy of the Honjin

"So?…"

For a while we sat around the brazier in silence, until finally Ginzo-san mustered some kind of response. His dismal tone reminded me of the dull thud of a pebble dropped into an empty well.

"And so?…" repeated Kindaichi-san. He alone was still smiling.

The inspector leaned forward.

"This means that Kenzo-san committed suicide?"

"That's correct."

"He killed Katsuko and then killed himself."

Ginzo-san's voice was filled with pain.

Ryuji-san hung his head.

"Yes, that's what happened," said Kindaichi-san. "That's why I had Doctor F— join us. Doctor, you were the first person to examine the two bodies. Tell me about Kenzo's wounds and the position of his body. Was it all consistent with the experiment we just watched?"

"If what you're asking is, is it possible that he inflicted wounds in several places on his own body before stabbing himself in the heart," I replied. "I'd say that if he'd set up the kind of device we've just seen, then, yes, it's perfectly possible."

"So there are no inconsistencies?"

"No, I don't think so. But the problem is: why?"

"He's right, Kindaichi-san," said Inspector Isokawa. "The question is why would Kenzo commit such a heinous act? To kill your bride and yourself on your wedding night? It's unthinkable. Why the hell did he do it?"

"Inspector, I think you might know why from our talk this morning with Shizuko Shiraki. I believe the fact that Katsuko wasn't a virgin might have had a direct bearing on this case."

The inspector glowered at Kindaichi-san.

"But—but, something so trivial… Because a woman isn't a virgin—if that was such a problem, then he could have broken off the engagement!"

"So you're saying he wouldn't have minded being a laughing stock among all his relatives? Well, you're right. An ordinary person could probably have endured such treatment. But Kenzo couldn't, and that was the cause of this terrible tragedy."

Kindaichi-san paused a moment.

"Inspector," he added, speaking very slowly, "this trick I just demonstrated for you, this was nothing. Most of the time you learn how a trick is done and say 'Aw'—it's a little disappointing, mere child's play. The true horror of this case isn't in the *way* it was done, but *why* it was done, and in order to understand that, it's necessary first to understand the man that Kenzo was—his personality, and most importantly, the atmosphere of the Ichiyanagi family in which he was raised."

He turned to look at Ryuji-san.

"We have Ryuji with us, the person who probably knew Kenzo the best. I am sure that he will correct me if anything I tell you is wrong. Last night I read all of Kenzo's diaries. What interested me more than its contents was the way

153

he handled them. Generally, a diary is something that you open at least once every day, three hundred and sixty-five times a year. It doesn't matter how meticulous someone may be, the binding is going to come a bit loose, the corners of the pages get a little bent. There may be smudges, or even here and there an ink blot or a fingerprint. But Kenzo's diaries have none of these. They're immaculate. They look as if they've just arrived from the bookshop, freshly bound, but if you think perhaps it was because he was neglecting to write in his diary, you'd be wrong. On the contrary, he was scrupulous about writing. Even his handwriting, every character, every pen stroke was unwavering, finely drawn. Looking at his calligraphy, it's so painstakingly perfect it leaves me short of breath. This alone gives me an image of Kenzo as sensitive, fastidious. I asked the maid, Kiyo, about it. Here is one example she gave me: she told me how one time a visitor came to the house in winter and she set up a brazier. The visitor's hand happened to graze the brazier slightly. After he left, Kenzo couldn't settle until that spot had been disinfected with alcohol. I would characterize this as an abnormal preoccupation with cleanliness. I'd go so far as to say Kenzo couldn't help feeling that all human beings other than himself were dirty, impure.

"There's one other personality trait that becomes clear from reading his diaries: he experienced intense emotional highs and lows; in other words he constantly went from extreme to extreme. His notions of love and hate were far from normal. With Kenzo, everything was exaggerated. There are no words to express how severe his case was. I realized this about him when I saw how casually he'd use a phrase like 'my mortal enemy'.

"The next thing that was unusual about the man was that he had a very strict sense of justice. In normal circumstances this might be considered a human virtue, but in Kenzo's case I think it should be considered one of his defects. It was merciless and it allowed for no flexibility whatsoever. He was hard on himself for any dishonesty or deceit, but he was also too strict with others. And then he had to grapple with the extra problem that by birth he was required to be a landowner with power over a whole community. This was at complete odds with his sense of justice, and his deep dislike of feudal ideology and practices.

"But the irony was that at the same time as abhorring the system, he could sometimes be the most haughtily aristocratic of all the Ichiyanagis. It was the result of being at once the powerful head of a clan, a descendant of the honjin and a large-scale landowner—when someone failed to show him respect, he was incredibly offended. In other words, Kenzo was a creature full of inconsistencies."

Ryuji-san had sat silently through Kindaichi-san's speech, staring down at the floor. The absence of any protest from him seemed to confirm each one of the points made. As his doctor, I had known Kenzo quite well, and felt Kindaichi-san was painting an accurate portrait of the man.

Kindaichi-san took up the story once more.

"A person such as this one had no choice but to be lonely. He couldn't trust anyone besides himself; indeed it would be fair to say that he considered everyone an enemy, and this attitude was even more pronounced when it came to his nearest relatives. The close relatives with whom Kenzo had regular daily contact were first of all his mother; and then his cousin Ryosuke; his youngest brother, Saburo; and finally his youngest sister, Suzuko. The latter two are barely more than children, so we can assume the people he had the most problems with were his mother and cousin, particularly Ryosuke.

"This Ryosuke-san is another very interesting character. At first sight he appears to be the exact opposite of Kenzo, personality-wise. On the surface he is meek, light-hearted, almost flippant, an easy man to get along with. But if you dig a little deeper you find he's not so different from Kenzo after all. He has quite a temper. It's all there in the diaries—how much trouble was caused to Kenzo by both Ryosuke and Itoko-san, how much they got on his nerves. The only reason this all never came to a head was because Kenzo prided himself on the self-control he learned through his superior education. Ryosuke knew this, and with feigned innocence would deliberately do things to rub Kenzo up the wrong way.

"And then into this situation came the issue of Katsuko. I don't need to remind anyone here of how much resistance there was to Kenzo and Katsuko's engagement. Kenzo forced them to accept it and the marriage finally happened. However, shortly before the wedding, Katsuko confessed to Kenzo that she wasn't a virgin, that she had once had a lover, but that wasn't all. She admitted that she had run into him recently, albeit accidentally. How did Kenzo react to this news?"

Kindaichi-san broke off here. Nobody offered a response. They all just sat there looking grim.

"I think that Kenzo was originally attracted by Katsuko's intelligence, her bright character. And there was also a calm within that brightness, something efficient and businesslike in her nature. These were all huge factors in her appeal for him, but I believe the aspect that held the greatest charm was that she appeared extremely virtuous. Purity was something that was of the utmost importance to Kenzo. And then, right before his wedding, he discovers that she has lain with another man. He believes that another man's blood runs inside her body. I told you earlier the story of how Kenzo had used alcohol to disinfect a heater that a guest's hand had accidentally touched, and now this! How can I say it?... Another man's— Well, to Kenzo all other people were dirty... The woman he held in his heart, the same woman he planned to hold in his arms, bring to his bed... For a man like Kenzo, just thinking about it would make his flesh crawl. He would have to break off the engagement. But unfortunately, Kenzo couldn't do that.

"To him, to back down and break the engagement in front of all the relatives that he had power over would be akin to removing his helmet and surrendering to the enemy. He could have taken Katsuko as his wife in name only, and deceived the eyes of his family, but there was a reason why he couldn't do that either. It was because just a few days before the wedding, Katsuko had met this man called Taya in a department store in Osaka. We have little idea of what kind of a man this Taya is, and of course Kenzo had none. But Taya may well have been the type to come and squeeze Kenzo for money to keep quiet about the affair. There was no guarantee at all that this wouldn't happen. For argument's sake, if he made Katsuko his wife in name only, glossing over the truth, imagine if Taya had then turned up. How shameful it would have been for Kenzo. Just picturing this, Kenzo decided he couldn't take the risk.

"Still, this wasn't just a way to solve a practical problem. I believe the origin of the motive lay much deeper, deep in Kenzo's psyche. He must have felt a furious hatred towards Katsuko for putting him in this hopeless position. This woman who with her defiled body was attempting to become his wife. It must have driven him to indescribable fury. But given Kenzo's personality, he would have avoided showing any part of this hatred and anger to Katsuko. Instead, the kind of outburst of emotion that both his father and his uncle had displayed was buried deep in Kenzo's heart and nagged at him persistently, eventually bursting out in the form of this sinister plan. The motive for this murder–suicide plan is incomprehensible to any normal person, but to the character of Kenzo, and in the eyes of such a family, proud descendants of a honjin, it becomes perfectly natural and reasonable. No, I'd go so far as to say that this was an unavoidable murder. Kenzo had to murder Katsuko; there was no other way. For appearances' sake, he had to go through with the wedding ceremony, given that he had insisted on it so forcefully, but he had absolutely no intention for them ever to live as a married couple. Thus there was no other possible moment for the killing than the point at which they were to consummate their marriage."

"So was it a double suicide?"

"A lovers' suicide?… No. I am sure it wasn't. This was a regular murder, fuelled by malice, hatred and fury at Katsuko for having entrapped him in this impossible situation… And he certainly succeeded in his plan to kill Katsuko. But this killer was very clever. He knew that however ingenious his murder plan, he was bound to get found out in the end. Or even if he wasn't found out, a man with such a conscience, such a strict sense of justice wouldn't be able to live with the knowledge that he was a murderer. Kenzo knew himself well. And so before the police could work it out, before his crime could register on his conscience, he killed himself, believing it was the right thing to do. In other words, this case is the opposite of the usual murder or detective story. In the normal order of things, first, there's a murder; second, the police or the private detective does their job; and then third, the murderer commits suicide upon being caught. This is the regular sequence of events. In our case, steps two and three were reversed. The murderer already killed himself, but that doesn't mean that we should take this case any more lightly as a result. From the start, the killer wanted to convince us that Katsuko's death wasn't his fault. He even tried to hide the fact of his own suicide. I hate to say it, but it's a very dirty trick."

"Not wanting it to look like suicide—was that from not wanting to admit defeat to his relatives? To not have his relatives, and Ryosuke in particular, ridicule him? Is that what he was thinking?"

"Right. Right. This whole puzzle, all of the mystery in this case came from that one thing. Lineage. The tragedy of the honjin."

CHAPTER 16

The Rehearsal

Nobody spoke for a long while. There was only the single brazier in the whole of the annexe house, and the cold was slowly seeping through our bones. But nobody wanted to leave, and thereby put an end to this conversation. The inspector was idly drawing *kanji* characters in the ashes, then erasing them, writing, erasing… Finally he looked up.

"Well, that explains more or less why all this happened, but how exactly did it happen? Tell us that."

Right away, Kindaichi-san's trademark grin and head scratch were back.

"Okay then, how about this? In this murder case, the perpetrator is already dead so we can't hear his confession. I suppose we're going to have to use our imagination. Luckily, we have assembled here a whole cast of people connected to the case. Let's go back to the beginning."

Kindaichi-san produced a small notebook from his pocket and opened it on his lap.

"The very first thing that struck me about this case was how much it resembled a mystery novel: starting, most obviously, with the locked room murder, then the introduction of the three-fingered man character, the sound of the koto, the photograph in the album and the burnt fragments of diary pages. All of these are straight out of the pages of a detective novel. If there were just one or two of these elements, perhaps I would have believed them to have been no more than coincidence, but with all these various elements carefully included, I couldn't help but believe it was part of a deliberate plan. And that was when I came across Saburo's mystery novels. Inspector, you will remember how thrilled I was to discover his collection."

Inspector Isokawa nodded.

"The trick at the centre of this case—making a suicide look like a murder—comes up quite often in detective fiction. The most famous example would be the one featured in the Sherlock Holmes story 'The Problem of Thor Bridge'. In order to make her suicide look like a murder, it was important for the perpetrator to get the weapon as far away from her body as possible. The weapon in this story was a revolver, to which she attached one end of a piece of string, then tied the other end to a heavy rock. The woman stood on top of Thor Bridge and shot herself in the head with the gun. The moment her hand loosened its grip on the revolver, the weight of the rock pulled it down to the bottom of the river below. I believe Kenzo came up with his plan after reading that story. The evidence is that the book was there among Saburo's collection, but unlike the rest of his books, some of the pages had been marked."

"I see," said Ryuji-san. "But then what was Saburo's role in this whole thing?"

Ryuji-san looked anxious, but Kindaichi-san just grinned and scratched his head.

"Wait a minute. I'm sure you're eager to know what part Saburo played, but if you don't mind, I'll come to that a little later. Suffice it to say that when Kenzo first began to hatch the plan, Saburo knew absolutely nothing about it. Given

161

Kenzo's personality, there seems little chance that he would have asked anyone else for help with such a serious undertaking. So keep this in mind as we follow how the plan developed and now let's take a look at the case once again, starting from the beginning and building it piece by piece."

Kindaichi-san looked at his notebook.

"Act one of this play took place on 23rd November—in other words, two days before the wedding—early in the evening. This is when the mysterious three-fingered man turned up at Kawada's tavern opposite the government office. That's the moment that the plan went into operation."

The inspector suddenly leaned forward.

"Really? But what relationship does the three-fingered man have to the Ichiyanagi family?"

"Inspector, that man had nothing whatsoever to do with the Ichiyanagis. He was no more than a traveller passing through."

"But, Ko-san—" Ginzo-san frowned. "He asked the okamisan the way to the Ichiyanagi residence."

"Yes, he did. But, Uncle, what he really wanted to know was the way to H— village. Inspector, you recall what happened this morning in K— when I asked at the tobacconist's?"

Inspector Isokawa's expression revealed that he had just figured it out. Kindaichi-san grinned.

"Everyone agrees that the man appeared to have come from far away. He most likely got off the train at N— station. There he asked for directions to H— village. So how do people usually reply when asked that question? H— is a good five miles from the station. It's much too difficult to give all the directions in one go, so people start by giving some of the landmarks along the route—you know: 'When you get to so-and-so, ask again'—it's perfectly normal. So the man reached K— town and did just that—asked again. I carried out my own little experiment this morning. The tobacconist who told me the way explained it something like this: 'If you follow this road, you'll end up in front of the government office in O—. When you get there, ask for the Ichiyanagi place. It's a huge mansion—you can't miss it. If you take the road that passes in front of the Ichiyanagi place it'll take you over the hill and into H—.' The three-fingered man was given the same kind of directions, and so when he got to O— government office, he asked the okamisan at the tavern opposite directions to the Ichiyanagi residence."

Inspector Isokawa, Ginzo-san and Ryuji-san all gave some version of a groan. It was a perfectly plausible explanation. The three-fingered man, with whom everyone had been obsessed, turned out to have only the scantest of connections to the Ichiyanagi family.

"I'm afraid it's true," continued Kindaichi-san. "Until that moment he had nothing to with the Ichiyanagis at all. But shortly after asking those directions, he was mixed up in the case. Or to be more precise, he got mixed up in Kenzo's plan. Next, he left the tavern and walked up here to the Ichiyanagi home. Just as everyone had said, it was a huge, impressive mansion. He had heard the okamisan and her customers talk about the head of the household getting married soon… so his interest was piqued and he peeped in through the gate. It was just normal human behaviour—natural curiosity. And when he was caught peeking by a local, to cover his embarrassment he asked again the way to H— village. This is still all totally normal behaviour. So asking the way to H— right then was to cover his embarrassment, but at the same time he simply said what was already in his mind. He'd always intended to go to H——. By the way, have you all noticed? From here, the road slopes sharply uphill. Everyone who saw him agrees that the three-fingered man was weak and emaciated. Before climbing the hill, he needed to take a break. But, aware that just the sight of him made people suspicious, he searched for somewhere out of sight—he clambered up into the thick bamboo on the cliff just behind the Ichiyanagi home. That makes perfect sense too."

"And then he ended up murdered by Kenzo," said the inspector.

This was my cue. I coughed politely to get Kindaichi-san's attention. He smiled at me.

"Not quite. I'd like to call on Doctor F—— to explain the next part. In fact, that's why I invited him to join us this evening. Doctor, could you give us the results of the autopsy?"

I nodded, understanding finally why he had asked me not to release the results until now. This young man was at first sight quite humble and modest, but in reality he enjoyed putting on a show. He'd wanted the information made public at the most dramatic moment possible.

"I'll explain the results of the autopsy as simply as I can. This man was not murdered. He died of natural causes. I can't ascertain the exact cause until there is a proper post-mortem, but in my opinion his heart most likely failed due to extreme fatigue and exhaustion. As for the injury to his chest area, that was made at least twenty-four hours after the time of death."

There were cries of surprise all around. Ryuji-san's eyes lit up and he leaned forward in excitement.

"So you're saying that my brother didn't kill this man?"

"That's right, he didn't," replied Kindaichi-san. "I always thought he hadn't. First of all, Kenzo was obsessed with his suicide plan and this three-fingered man was not originally part of it, and second, he wouldn't have committed the injustice of murdering a completely innocent bystander."

"But that injury? The one in his chest…"

"Well, Inspector, those are the results of Kenzo's practice run. Just like I did earlier this evening, Kenzo also performed an experiment. He devised the plan, but he had no idea whether it would work or not, and even if it did work, how much time he would need to complete it. So he practised. And he used that corpse for his dry run. Uncle, you mentioned that on the night before the murder Suzuko said she'd heard a sound like koto strings being plucked. That was Kenzo rehearsing."

We exchanged looks. Ryuji-san had turned pale again. This wasn't news of another murder, but it was just as dreadful— or rather, it was more dreadful—it was downright macabre. Shivers ran up and down my spine.

"To get back to the story of the three-fingered man—after he climbed up the cliff behind the annexe house, it wasn't long before he breathed his last. It was Kenzo who found him. That was the night of the 23rd or the morning of the 24th, and Kenzo probably couldn't believe his luck—here was a perfect guinea pig for his experiment. He secretly carried the body down to the annexe house and hid it away. As you may have guessed, he used that closet behind the tokonoma for a hiding place. That explains why the man's fingerprints were in there.

"And that concludes the events of the night of the 23rd. Then the next night was the 24th, the day before the wedding.

You may recall that there was a heated exchange in the sitting room of the main house that day. Kenzo and his mother quarrelled about the koto. In the middle of the argument, Ryosuke turned up with the coffin he'd made for the cat, and Saburo arrived back from the barber's shop in the village. Saburo revealed that the three-fingered man had been asking the way to the Ichiyanagi house. When she heard about the man having three fingers, Suzuko was reminded of a koto. For Suzuko it was a very reasonable association, and she pretended to play. This all had a crucial connection to the case. What it did was to give Kenzo an important idea."

We all looked confused.

"Kenzo had already laid down the details of his plan, but he still hadn't worked out what kind of string to use. It had to be thin yet strong, and he needed a great length of it. While he was still puzzling over the question, Suzuko mimed a three-fingered man playing the koto. Now, I want you to remember that at this point in time, the three-fingered man was already dead and stashed in the closet at the annexe house. Kenzo must have been truly surprised when the very man he was planning to use in his practice run suddenly became the topic of conversation in his family's sitting room. At the same time, watching Suzuko's hand, he had a flash of inspiration. Three fingers and a koto… right there it came to him. Kenzo thought of using a length of koto string. It's ironic that such an innocent, simple-minded young girl through such a harmless gesture could have had such a major influence on a murder. It's really quite awful, but it's true. Kenzo went straight to the storehouse and found a length of koto string. In this house, there are so many kotos that there's a surplus of spare string. No one would notice if some of it

166

went missing. While Kenzo was in the storehouse looking for the string, the koto bridges on the Lovebird caught his eye. I don't believe Kenzo was originally going to use a koto bridge to make the vertex point on the lavatory roof. I imagine he planned to use a forked twig or something, but when he saw the arched shape of the koto bridges, he realized it was of course the perfect device to support the string, and he took one. And that is how the murder case ended up having such a deep connection to that musical instrument."

The inspector murmured his acknowledgement.

"And then he rehearsed the trick that night?" said Ginzo-san.

"He did, and there were two results that he hadn't expected. The first was that the string rubbed against lots of the branches in the bamboo thicket and made a pinging noise. He realized that if he didn't cut down some of the bamboo, the same thing would happen the following evening. However, Kenzo didn't feel like going out and cutting down trees, so he decided to let the sound be produced again, but this time to camouflage it. So between murdering Katsuko and killing himself, he plucked wildly at the koto in the room. The other members of the Ichiyanagi household were awakened by those sounds and remained oblivious to the other camouflaged sounds of the string running through the bamboo thicket."

"Huh," said the inspector.

"And what was the second unexpected result of the experiment?" asked Ginzo-san.

"That Saburo discovered it. Well, that's my hypothesis— that at some point, Saburo got in on the plan."

This came as a surprise to everyone. Ryuji-san's face was ashen.

CHAPTER 17

The Accidental Locked Room

"And so, if I guessed rightly, what effect did Saburo's discovery of the experiment have? Well, we won't know for sure until we ask Saburo himself. However, I think the nature of some of the tricks demonstrates that he must have been involved. There were a lot of games played. I would go so far as to claim that Kenzo would have been satisfied to make it look like a double murder, but it hadn't occurred to him to try to frame someone for the crime. Here, the aficionado of detective novels became involved. Saburo decided that a murder without a murderer didn't cut it, and quickly devised a fake one. The deceased three-fingered man was the perfect scapegoat. Neither Kenzo nor Saburo had any idea who this man was, nor why he'd been asking directions to the Ichiyanagi house, but he was shady-looking and he had after all been asking about their home. Additionally, Saburo had guessed that the man's three-fingered handprint had probably been left on the glass at Kawada's tavern, and this awoke his creative urge. Any fan of mystery novels could come up with the idea of planting fingerprints. But that wasn't enough for Saburo. The photograph in the album, the fragments of diary pages, all were to create the impression of some kind of bad blood between Kenzo and the three-fingered man. These are tricks straight out of the mind of a crime novel enthusiast. The murder–suicide plan was created from a melding of the brilliant scientific mind of Kenzo and the widely read Saburo's, which is what made it such a complex case to figure out. In conclusion, the case was a collaborative project between these two."

"So why was the photo there in the album?"

"Inspector, you cut the photo out along with the cardboard page. If you had tried to remove it from the page we would have spotted the trick right away. Look!…"

Kindaichi-san picked up the photo which he'd already removed from its cardboard backing.

"On the back of this photograph, you can see traces of where it was peeled away from its previous location. Also, once I removed the backing, it became clear that a different picture used to be attached to that page of the album. Saburo had carefully removed the original photo from its spot in the album and replaced it with this one. In other words, Kenzo's mortal enemy, whom he swore to hate all his life, existed but it wasn't the man in this photo."

"Where did Saburo get hold of this photograph?"

"The three-fingered man was carrying it of course."

"But that doesn't make sense," said Ryuji-san. "People don't usually go around carrying their own photograph."

"That's true. Just as you say. Normally. But there are people in some lines of work who always have their own picture on them—bus and taxi drivers for example."

Inspector Isokawa suddenly cried out.

"That's right. I'd been thinking the same thing—that I've seen photos like this one all over. It's the type of photo that drivers have on their licences."

"That's it. Exactly," said Kindaichi-san delightedly, scratching at his bird's-nest head. "And knowing that, it explains the terrible gash on that man's face and his two missing fingers. Incidentally, I have discovered who he was. His name is Kyokichi Shimizu. He was born in Shitsuki-gun, and moved to Tokyo when he was a young boy. Later he took up work as a taxi driver. Fairly recently his car was involved in a serious accident, and that was how he got those injuries. Obviously he could no longer work as a driver, and wanting to spend some time convalescing, he wrote a letter to his aunt in H— village asking to stay with her for a while. She wrote back to say yes, but hadn't heard anything from him since. She'd assumed he was on his way and had been expecting him to arrive yesterday or today. That's what I heard from Sergeant Kimura after I sent him to make some door-to-door enquiries in H—. According to his aunt, Kyokichi Shimizu had never been to this part of the country before. And when Sergeant Kimura showed her this photo, she said that she hadn't seen him since he was a young boy, so she couldn't say for sure if it was him or not. But then she added that the man in the photo looked a lot like her brother—Kyokichi's father—so that it was probably him after all. To sum up, the three-fingered man was Kyokichi Shimizu, professional taxi driver, who, on his way to his aunt's home in H— village, suffered an unhappy end to his life on the cliff behind this house."

"And then his death was used by my brother."

Ryuji-san looked sorrowful but the inspector paid him no heed.

"And what about the burnt pages from the diaries? How do you explain those?"

"That was another one of Saburo's tricks," said Kindaichi-san with a chuckle. "For years on end Kenzo had kept a scrupulous record of everything he'd done. There was bound to be something among his many experiences worth using. Saburo pulled out bits from several places and made a kind of montage. Here's the outline of the plot. Take a look."

From between the pages of his notebook, Kindaichi-san produced the five fragments of burnt paper.

"Starting with the fragment labelled number one:

...on my way to the beach I went by the usual place. Ofuyu-san was playing the koto again. Lately I find the sound of that koto melancholy...

"And number three:

...Ofuyu-san's funeral. A desolate, mournful day. It's drizzling again here on the island. The funeral was...

"And if we follow that with number five:

...before I left the island, I paid one more visit to Ofuyu-san's grave. I took some wild chrysanthemums and, as I was praying, I thought I could hear the sound of a koto. Abruptly I...

"From the condition of the pen and the colour of the ink, and as they all feature the same woman, Ofuyu-san, it's clear that these three sections were all written at the same time. However, number two:

...that dog, that brute. I really despise him. I will despise that man for the rest of my life...

"And number four:

...I'm thinking of challenging him to a duel. This inexpressible
fury. When I think of the lonely death that she met, I could tear
him limb from limb. I consider him my mortal enemy and I hate
him, hate him, hate h...

"These sections were written with a different pen, in a slightly different shade of ink. I believe that sections one, three and five were written by Kenzo during his travels, and none of them with a fountain pen. Sections two and four were written at a completely different time. From the penmanship and other features, I'm convinced that they were written a while before the other three. Probably from when Kenzo was still working at the university. Ryuji-san, do you have any memory of that time?"

Ryuji-san looked up suddenly. It was clear he had remembered something. But just as quickly he looked down again, unable to hold anyone's gaze. After some hesitation, he began to tell a story:

"It was a very strange thing. While he was working at the university, there was some kind of an incident, and afterwards my brother felt extremely resentful towards one of his colleagues. In fact, he hated him. This man used to be a close friend of his, but they fell out over the daughter of a teacher that they both knew well. Kenzo was completely betrayed by his friend, double-crossed... or at least that's what he believed. It resulted in my brother being left in a shameful position, and he was forced to leave his post at the university. The young woman fell sick, presumably as a result of this incident, and eventually died. I don't know how much of that is true, I don't have all the facts of the case, but Kenzo wholeheartedly believed that his former friend was entirely at fault. My brother was a person of such extreme moods that he loathed this man to the very core of his being. When the phrase 'my mortal enemy' came up in this case, I immediately thought of that person, but then we were told that this mortal enemy was someone he had met on an island, so I assumed it couldn't be him after all. What's more, this is a man whose name is immediately recognizable. These days he's a famous scholar. I couldn't believe that a man like that could have— Anyway, that's why I didn't say anything until now."

"I see. And did you ever meet this man?"

"Never. I sometimes see his photo in the papers, but only in recent years. Honestly, I couldn't tell whether the photo you showed us from the album was him in his younger years or not."

"That's completely understandable. Saburo was quite ingenious in the way he combined that incident with the later episode from Kenzo's time on the island. Then by working in the photo of the three-fingered man, he created a clever piece of fiction for us. Quite a job."

Kindaichi-san laughed.

"He even chose the piece from the island because it featured a koto. Kenzo was the kind of person who would never show his diary to another person. But he was no match for Saburo. Saburo had often amused himself by poking his nose into his brother's private affairs. And he clearly had a good brain, being able to recall immediately what Kenzo had written about and when, where to find it, and how to rearrange it. Therefore, I believe that from the moment Saburo joined the planning, it was his mind that devised the scheme, and Kenzo became no more than a puppet following orders. Saburo was showing off his vast knowledge of detective fiction and Kenzo was no match for all that knowledge."

I didn't think Kindaichi-san's theory too outlandish. With the exception of Ryuji-san, who had always seemed to me a fairly normal person, I knew that the whole Ichiyanagi clan was very eccentric.

"And then after the plan was concocted, they cut off the corpse's hand and buried the rest of the body in the charcoal kiln. That was before sunrise on the 25th. But somehow later that evening, right before the wedding ceremony was due to start, the three-fingered man made an appearance at the kitchen door. I believe that was actually Kenzo dressed up to look like him. He and Saburo had set up the trick with the photo album, but if for some reason it escaped the notice of the police, then the misdirection wouldn't work, so they devised this piece of theatre, which couldn't fail to capture the attention of the investigators, and was intended to make everyone believe that the three-fingered man was still alive on the day of the murder. After leaving the kitchen, still dressed in the three-fingered man's clothing, Kenzo took the path from the west side of the property, ran along the north side of the cliff, and then slid down the hillside just behind the annexe house. He slipped into the house, where he changed back into his usual clothes and waited for Akiko to turn up with the scrap of paper and hand it to him. He tore it into shreds in front of her, stuck the pieces into the pocket in the sleeve of his kimono, and then as he left the annexe, he made a point of asking Akiko to close all the rain shutters. When Akiko finally got back to the main house, Kenzo was nowhere to be seen. The reason no one could find him was that he had returned to the annexe house, and was making the fake footprints; cutting himself and taking some of his own blood to leave the three-fingered handprints on the pillar and the inside of the rain shutter; taking the shoes and the other clothes belonging to the three-fingered man and shoving them into the chimney of the charcoal kiln; and then finally pulling the end of the prepared koto string through the gap in the ranma transom."

"Kindaichi-san," said Inspector Isokawa, "you're saying that the fingerprints were already there from early in the evening?"

"They were. There's no other time that he would have been able to make them. That was the first clue I had to solving this case. It was those bloody fingerprints—there were other prints in more obvious places, such as the folding screen, but those were made by fingers wearing koto picks. In contrast, the clearer fingerprints were left in more difficult to find locations. I thought there must be something significant about that. This suggested two things to me. The fingerprints in these two locations (the pillar and the rain shutter) were discovered a long time after the others, and I was sure the killer had counted on that. In other words, it would have been disadvantageous to the killer if the investigators had found them any earlier. It didn't matter that they were found, just that they shouldn't be found quickly. So why? I deduced that they must have had a different appearance to the other fingerprints, due to how dry they already were. If they'd been found too early, the discrepancy between the colour of those prints and the other ones would have been obvious. I concluded that it was better for the killer that they were found as late as possible. The second point was that these two spots were concealed well enough for there to have been fingerprints there during earlier activity in the annexe house, such as the sake cup ceremony. But even before that, I found it strange that a criminal who was cautious enough to put koto picks over his fingers would also be careless enough to leave his fingerprints all over the place. So I came to the conclusion that those fingerprints must have been left deliberately, and moreover long before the crime was committed."

"Hah!"

The inspector sounded impressed.

Kindaichi-san grinned.

"And now the stage was set. Kenzo took the severed hand to the main house. Now you might ask why—considering Kenzo had gone to the effort of taking the shoes and the clothes up to the charcoal kiln—hadn't he disposed of the hand at the same time? I believe he was following Saburo's instructions. I think Saburo was enjoying himself far too much. He probably couldn't resist using the hand for some nefarious purpose of his own, so he got Kenzo to leave it in a hiding place for him to pick up later. Of course, Saburo didn't want to keep it himself. He had to be prepared in case the house was searched after the murder. He hit on the idea of getting Kenzo to put it in the cat's coffin that he knew Suzuko had hidden in her room. And as he had hoped, right after the murder Suzuko took the coffin out and buried it, making it the perfect hiding place."

"And after that Kenzo went to the study and dealt with the diaries?"

"Yes, that's right. Probably Saburo had already marked which passages should be used. All Kenzo had to do was tear out the pages and partially burn them—along with the scraps of the letter in his kimono sleeve. However, as we know, he didn't burn those scraps, he didn't get rid of a single piece, just kept them in his sleeve... There's no doubt that with

176

someone as scrupulous as Kenzo, he must have left those scraps there purposely so we would 'find' the letter from his so-called mortal enemy.

"Then shortly afterwards, the wedding ceremony began. Here there were two circumstances of note. The first was that the koto was moved to the annexe house. Luckily for Kenzo's plan, the mayor made that suggestion. If no one had brought up the subject, Kenzo surely planned to do so. He was quick to tell Katsuko that the koto was hers.

"The second thing of importance was that Kenzo told Saburo to accompany Great-Uncle Ihei home. It was purely to give Saburo an alibi for the murder. By the way, I have a question for you, Ryuji-san."

Ryuji-san raised an eyebrow.

"I'm sure the inspector here has already asked you the same question, but I know that you were already here on the evening of the 25th. That being the case, why didn't you attend your brother's wedding ceremony? And why the next morning did you pretend to have just arrived?"

Ryuji-san looked pained.

"First, I have to say that only now do I understand why... Kenzo strictly forbade me to come back from Osaka for the wedding. I guess he didn't want me to fall under suspicion, so he was making sure I had an ironclad alibi. Of course I had no idea of his motives, but the tone of the letter he wrote me made me extremely worried and I felt I had to come. So I left the conference one day early and came to K— town to find out what was going on. I thought it was better not to show my face at the wedding, so I stayed away. But then the next day there was all the commotion, so I met up with Saburo and Great-Uncle Ihei and arrived at the house in the morning."

"Your big brother really loved you, didn't he?"

"I'm fairly sure he wasn't acting out of love. I think it was because I was the only person who really understood him."

"I get it. He was less afraid of your falling under suspicion for his murder than of your reading his true intentions."

Ryuji-san nodded.

"That's probably true. That morning, as soon as I heard what happened, I immediately thought my brother had done it. Why he did it, and how he could have done it, those were the things I couldn't fathom."

"I'd like to thank you. That clears up what you were doing here. Next, the scene of the crime. The sake ceremony had just finished and Kenzo had covertly taken a koto bridge from the Lovebird and slipped it into the sleeve pocket of his mother's kimono. I guessed that from what you told me, Inspector Isokawa. How did I work it out? Well, the koto bridge that we found in the pile of leaves had no other fingerprints on it besides the three-fingered man's. That means it couldn't possibly have been one of the bridges attached to the koto that night. That evening, both Suzuko and Katsuko had played the Lovebird koto. Every koto player takes a few moments before playing to tune the instrument, adjusting the position of the bridges with their left hand. If the koto bridge we found outside the annexe house had been taken from that instrument, it goes without saying that it would have both Suzuko's *and* Katsuko's fingerprints on it. It would be pointless for the killer to wipe off another person's fingerprints and then put his own on the koto bridge instead. So it stands to reason that the bridge we found in the pile of leaves outside was never on that particular koto that evening. It had been removed from the koto while still in the storehouse and the bloody fingerprint added to it before it was used in the commission of the crime."

Ginzo-san nodded calmly and puffed on his pipe. Ryuji-san was still staring at the floor.

"I discovered the koto bridge that had really been on the koto that night, the one that Kenzo had taken from the instrument after Katsuko finished playing, still in his mother's kimono sleeve pocket. I'm guessing that Saburo was supposed to have got rid of it later, but Kenzo didn't get around to telling him. Or perhaps Saburo just forgot about it in all the confusion following the discovery of the murder. Anyway, it stayed inside the pocket until today.

"I believe I've covered all the preparations; now we come to the moment of the tragedy…"

Kindaichi-san's expression darkened. We all found ourselves holding our breath.

"It's an atrocious crime, and the fact that it was planned and thought through down to the last detail makes it even more terrible. Did Kenzo lie motionless in the marriage bed waiting for that waterwheel to start turning? And when he heard the sound of it starting up, did he leap to his feet, and, pretending to head towards the lavatory, fetch the katana from the closet? Then after slashing Katsuko to death with that sword, he put three koto picks onto his fingers, played some chords on the koto and rubbed bloody traces of the koto picks onto the folding screen. I admit that the fact that he left those koto-pick traces on the screen gives me a grim sense of satisfaction. Not because Kenzo used the picks to conceal his own fingerprints but because it displays his meticulous nature. He'd already used koto string and koto bridges. It was fitting that he should use koto picks too. I feel that was his reasoning. Next, he pulled off the koto picks at the washbasin, and on his way back, took hold of the end of the string that was hanging through the ranma, pulling it with him back to the tatami room. Then he killed himself in the way that I demonstrated to you earlier. And that was how the mysterious Honjin Murder was committed."

Everyone stayed silent, lost in their own thoughts. The cold had seeped into my core and I gave an involuntary shudder. Right away, as if the contagion had spread, the rest of the assembled guests began to shiver. That was when Ryuji-san suddenly spoke up:

"But what I don't understand is why my brother didn't just leave the rain shutters open. It would have looked as if the murderer had got in and out that way. Surely that would have seemed more natural?"

Kindaichi-san's reaction was dramatic. He began to scratch away in that knotted thatch of hair with passionate abandon. When he spoke, his stammer was more pronounced than ever.

"Th-That's th-the m-m-most fascinating part of this case—"

He grabbed his cup and downed the dregs of his tea. Then he continued in a calmer voice.

"That's exactly what he was supposed to do. But something unexpected happened—something that completely threw off the plan. Circumstances that he had never imagined... It snowed. Just imagine—he'd planted a trail of footprints—the same ones that he had leading into the front door—but heading away from the building through the garden to the west. The idea was to suggest that the killer had escaped that way after the murder. But the trail of footprints was completely buried by the snow. Should he make a new trail? But that was impossible. For one thing, he had already got rid of the three-fingered man's worn-out old shoes in the chimney of the charcoal kiln. Likewise, there was no point in opening the rain shutters now to suggest the killer escaped that way, but then leaving the snow completely untouched outside. There was nothing for it but to turn the crime into a locked room murder scene— Well, we can't know for sure exactly how he reasoned, but I think that was why he left the rain shutters locked. In other words, what we have here was not after all a meticulously planned locked room murder, but a case where the killer was reluctantly forced to create one. In other words, an accidental locked room murder mystery."

(THIS CONCLUDES DOCTOR F—'S NOTES)

CHAPTER 18

Red Spider Lilies

That concludes Doctor F—'s report. He did make some further notes regarding Saburo's involvement in the case, but I have obtained that information from other sources, and I will attempt to summarize it myself.

Once Saburo had recovered from his tetanus infection, Inspector Isokawa grilled him about his role in the case. He confessed everything, and it was more or less exactly as Kosuke Kindaichi had predicted. He'd got mixed up in the plan when he'd discovered his brother performing his dry run. This is how Saburo told it:

"I'll never forget that menacing look on my brother's face… That night I noticed there was a light on in the annexe house, so I tiptoed up to take a look. My brother had been in a strange mood for days. He'd been in another world, deep in thought about something, and easily startled by the slightest noise. It had been most obvious that afternoon when I'd got back from the barber's and told everyone about the three-fingered man. I saw his expression change. This was fresh in my mind, so when I saw the light on in the house I just had to go and see what he was up to. The garden gate was tightly locked with the bolt pulled across on the inside, so I climbed over the fence to get into the annexe grounds. I crept around to the west side and spied on him through a small gap between the rain shutters. Imagine my shock when a katana

suddenly came through the ranma above my head! I would
have screamed, but in the terror of the moment I couldn't
speak. I stood there, dumbstruck, as the sword hung there in
the air. Then a few moments later it began to make that *ping
ping twang* sound before flying up in the air and landing on the
ground by the stone lantern. Right at the moment it landed,
the rain shutters opened and my brother's face appeared. It
all happened too quickly for me to think to hide myself, and
so Kenzo found me standing there like a fool. The expression
of fury on his face—I'll never forget it. He grabbed me by the
scruff of my neck and dragged me into the house, where I
found the three-fingered man lying dead on the tatami. And
with that gory wound in his chest—"

Even Saburo couldn't help trembling when he recalled
the ghastly scene.

"I was convinced that my brother had taken leave of his
senses, and that I was about to meet the same fate as the
man on the tatami. Kenzo was worked up and held me so
tightly that for a while I couldn't even breathe. But gradually he got less agitated, and like a balloon releasing air,
he sort of deflated. In fact, I had never seen my brother so
dejected. Kenzo was always weak, he always used to brood over
things like a girl, but he never showed that side of himself
in everyday life. He always came across as cold-hearted and
haughty. To see him so low, with no pride or honour left,
frankly I felt sorry for him, but at the same time it gave me
a kind of thrill…

"Finally, Kenzo managed to pull himself together, and
began to tell me about his plan, but only part of it. He was
almost in tears when he begged me not to say a word to anybody. The reason I say only part of his plan, is that he never

mentioned Katsuko-san to me at all—just that he planned to kill himself but he didn't want it to look like suicide. It had to look like murder. Of course, I was horrified and told him he couldn't do that. So he asked me why not."

Saburo's reply to that question of Kenzo's was remarkable and somewhat chilling; proof that he was indeed a true fanatic of the detective novel genre.

"This is what I told Kenzo. When a murder is committed, the prime suspect is the one with the most to gain. In the case of Kenzo's death, that would be whoever inherited the Ichiyanagi family estate—in our case, my older brother, Ryuji. But as Ryuji was nowhere near at the time, he wouldn't be on the list of suspects. I told him suspicion would fall on me instead. He asked me, 'Why? Why would anyone suspect you? You'd hardly benefit at all from my death. All of this property would pass to Ryuji.' I answered, 'That's not quite accurate. If you die, I'll inherit fifty thousand yen in insurance money'…"

Kenzo's face must have been a picture when Saburo explained this. I'm sure he stared at him as if he were seeing some kind of alien monster.

"Eventually though, according to Saburo, Kenzo's face broke into a ghastly grimace and his tone changed.

"'Saburo, you're a clever one, aren't you? You have quite a head on your shoulders. Right, then go ahead—tell everyone that it wasn't murder, that I killed myself. But if you do, you won't be able to collect a single yen of insurance money. You do realize that when it turns out that the deceased has committed suicide, there's no payout on the insurance? Is that what you want? To throw away your chance to get your hands on fifty thousand yen? You're not as smart as you thought, are you?'"

Older brothers, younger brothers alike, every member of the Ichiyanagi house was peculiar in some way, but Saburo was for sure the most freakish of them all. After hearing Kenzo's explanation, he must have found himself in a terrible dilemma. But he came up with a solution favourable to himself: in order to be free of suspicion of Kenzo's murder, he made his brother promise to manufacture an alibi for him. Once he'd extracted this promise he was in a fine mood, devoting himself to the plan and drawing on his extensive knowledge of detective novels.

I believe that the reason Saburo was so enthusiastic about helping his brother with the plan was of course in order to be sure to get his fifty thousand yen, but also because this was the first time in his life that he was able to feel superior to his big brother in any way. He was revelling in it. As Kosuke Kindaichi also pointed out, the more Saburo became involved, or the more the plot became similar to that of a detective novel, the more the status of the two brothers switched. Kenzo quite readily followed all of Saburo's commands. Every bizarre trick that Saburo came up with, he'd give a bitter smile and follow his orders. This was Saburo's forte, and he must have been having the time of his life.

The ruse with the three-fingered man's photo, as well as the stunt with the burnt diary pages—these were all Saburo's ideas. Needless to say, the idea of cutting off the corpse's hand to use for fingerprints was his as well. To be fair, the scheme to frame the three-fingered man for the murder had already been in Kenzo's mind, but he had not come up with a precise plan of how to achieve that. He had the vague notion that if he buried the body where no one would find it, then eventually suspicion would fall on the three-fingered man...

that was as far as he'd got. Saburo took over, embellishing and improving, and staging the performance to perfection.

There are people in the world with such a talent, and Saburo was certainly one of those. Rather than taking on the leading role themselves, they are able to take the outline of a script written by another and embellish it, edit it, offer advice and suggestions, and turn it into a fascinating piece of theatre.

However, in the case of this murder–suicide, Saburo ended up going beyond his role of stage director. He just couldn't help getting a little more involved. The situation played so much to his strengths, that in the end he just had to put himself centre stage too. He explained it this way…

"I planned to use the severed hand again if anyone at all had suspected suicide. I got Kenzo to hide it in the coffin so it would be buried along with the cat. Then the next night I snuck out to dig it up again. That was when Suzuko had her sleepwalking episode. I looked up and saw her staggering towards me. I held out the severed hand with its three fingers to scare her.

But, you know, I'd never dreamed of having to use the hand to do the same trick again. It was that meddling, jumped-up Kosuke Kindaichi who forced me into it. If he'd been a more serious, dignified kind of detective, I never would have acted so childishly. But he turned up, just about the same age as me, looking so scruffy, with that feeble stammer. It got right up my nose that he was swanning around pretending to be a detective. Then he came and told me that mechanical tricks in locked room murders were boring. He challenged me. Thinking back, I realize now that this was a deliberate strategy, and I fell right into his trap…

"Anyway, I just had to show him. I made up my mind to demonstrate my locked room murder trick one more time. I took the hand I'd dug up the night before, dipped it in my own blood and made more fingerprints on the folding screen. Then I took it and reburied it in the cat's grave. After that, I put on the performance for him. Obviously, I didn't mean to cut myself so deeply. I intended just to graze myself lightly with the sword. I performed the same steps that my brother did, then stuck the sword into the folding screen and tried to cut myself from behind, but I miscalculated somehow and I gave myself a deep gash instead. If you take a look at the camphor tree in the garden, you'll find the razor I used instead of a sickle."

The long and short of it is that this young man, Saburo, was something of a psychopath. To him, flirting with death was an amusing game. To the very end, he insisted that he had never had the slightest idea that Kenzo planned to murder Katsuko. This may well have been the truth. But who's to say even if he had known, he wouldn't have done exactly the same thing? Would it have made him hesitate at all?

Saburo was of course charged, but while he was waiting for judgement to be handed down, the political situation in Japan worsened. He was called up to fight in China, where he eventually died in battle. Sweet young Suzuko also passed away the following year. But perhaps it was a blessing that she did. Last year, their cousin Ryosuke went on a trip to Hiroshima, and was unlucky enough to be there when the atomic bomb was dropped. The village elders noted that this was also the city in which his father had died. They wondered aloud if this wasn't some sort of fate. War, having taken the father, had finally taken the son as well.

Ryuji stuck out the war in Osaka. He refused to be evacuated to his home village. He'd never liked village life, and ever since the murder case, he'd had enough of the old way, the life of a family of the honjin. These days, that grand Ichiyanagi residence is occupied by the dowager Itoko, along with her elder daughter Taeko, who recently made it back from Shanghai with no more than the clothes on her back. The branch family house is still home to Ryosuke's widow, Akiko, and their three children, but the gossip in the village is that no one sees eye to eye about anything, and that the arguments are never-ending.

And those are the facts of the Honjin Murder Case. I must confess that I never intended to mislead my readers. I explained from the outset the location of the waterwheel. Moreover, right in the opening chapter of this book, I wrote the following:

I feel I owe a debt of gratitude to the killer for devising such a fiendish method to stab this man and woman.

Of course, the man and woman I was referring to were the three-fingered man, Kyokichi Shimizu, and the bride, Katsuko. Katsuko was of course stabbed to death, whereas Kyokichi was merely stabbed. I purposely refrained from writing, "who brutally killed a man and a woman". If you, dear reader, assumed that I was referring to Kenzo and Katsuko, then that is entirely your responsibility.

In the same chapter when describing the crime scene, I wrote:

…the couple lying there, soaked in the crimson of their own blood

I wrote "soaked in their own blood", but never did I specify that they had both been murdered. I learned these devices from my own reading of detective novels, specifically Agatha Christie's *The Murder of Roger Ackroyd*.

And so in closing: as I was completing this manuscript, I paid one last visit to the Ichiyanagi residence.

On my earlier visit, there had still been the chill of early spring in the air, and not a single shoot of green in sight anywhere. The ridges of earth in the rice fields had been bare. But now it was autumn, and as far as the eye could see, there were golden waves of ripening rice. I passed once again by the broken waterwheel, and climbed the cliff that marked the northern border of the property. I scrambled my way through the thick bamboo, and finally had a southerly view over the residence.

According to my sources, the property taxes, along with the new agrarian reforms, had affected even the Ichiyanagi family, and they had been unable to ward off financial ruin. Perhaps it was a stretch of my imagination, but as I looked out over that once-grand home sitting in the shadow of the honjin, I fancied I smelled the odour of decay.

I turned my eyes slightly to look at the spot on the northeastern edge of the property where, ten years earlier, Suzuko had buried her beloved pet kitten. The ground was carpeted in those deep red spider lilies sometimes known as equinox flowers. I couldn't help imagining they were soaked in the blood of poor, sweet Suzuko.

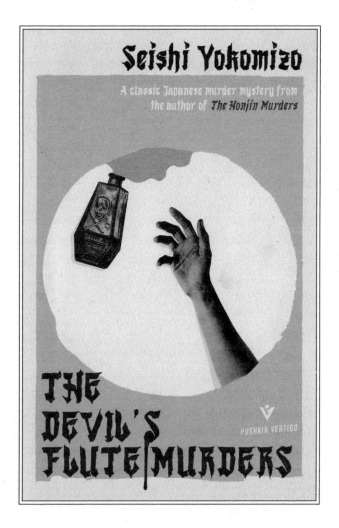

Seishi Yokomizo

A classic Japanese murder mystery from
the author of *The Honjin Murders*

THE
DEVIL'S
FLUTE MURDERS

PUSHKIN VERTIGO